CAPTIV

Eight years ago, Emma and Jordan had been wildly in love—but then suddenly Jordan's attitude had changed and he had thrown her out of his life. Now he had come back again, saying he still loved her—but what could she do about it? For now she was married to David, who had more claim to her loyalty than Jordan ever would . . .

Books you will enjoy
by ANNE MATHER

FOLLOW THY DESIRE

On the day of her wedding, Helen realised that she could not go through with it—not now that she had met Barry's half-brother Morgan. So instead she accepted Morgan's invitation to go back with him to Africa and look after his young daughter. But Morgan had not mentioned marriage, and in fact had made it clear that the job was all he was offering her. Was Helen making a complete fool of herself—or worse?

SCORPIONS' DANCE

Miranda had married Jaime Knevett purely to make use of him, and theirs had never been a true marriage; in fact they had not seen each other for four years. Now Miranda had come to Brazil to ask Jaime for an annulment. But was that what she really wanted?

ROOTED IN DISHONOUR

Beth was genuinely fond of Willard Petrie, which was why she had agreed to marry him and go to live in his Caribbean island home. But 'genuinely fond' was hardly the way to describe how she had begun to feel about Raoul Valerian. Could she fight the feeling and remain loyal to Willard?

LOREN'S BABY

Caryn just couldn't be sure whether or not Tristan Ross was the father of her dead sister Loren's baby. Surely Loren had been telling the truth? Tristan denied it, yet he was making himself responsible for the child, wasn't he? And then Caryn found herself faced with another problem . . .

CAPTIVE DESTINY

BY

ANNE MATHER

MILLS & BOON LIMITED
17–19 FOLEY STREET
LONDON W1A 1DR

First published 1978
Australian copyright 1978
Philippine copyright 1978
This edition 1978

© Anne Mather 1978

ISBN 0 263 72836 6

Set in Linotype Plantin 10 on 11½ pt.

Made and printed in Great Britain by
Richard Clay (The Chaucer Press), Ltd., Bungay, Suffolk

CHAPTER ONE

THE telephone rang and Emma picked up the receiver.

'Avery Antiques. Can I help——' she was beginning, when a harsh, masculine voice interrupted her.

'Emma! How are you?'

Her heart quickened its beat for a moment and then she squashed the sudden anger that gripped her. There was no point in expending unnecessary emotion needlessly. She ought to be able to speak to Jordan without feeling anything at all, but it wasn't easy when for so long resentment had coloured her reactions towards him.

'Good morning, Jordan,' she responded now, coolly, without expression. 'What can I do for you?'

'So formal!' he remarked cynically. 'I asked how you were.'

'Oh—well, I'm fine, thank you.' Emma's fingers tightened on the receiver. It wasn't like Jordan to care, one way or the other.

'You are? Good.' She could hear the irony in his tone. There was a long pause, then: 'Aren't you going to ask how I am?'

I don't particularly care! But the words were never spoken. Instead, she said: 'I am rather busy at the moment, Jordan. If there's something——'

'There is.' His crisp tones overrode her polite rejection. 'Have dinner with me this evening.'

'No!' The refusal was out before she had time to formulate her feelings. 'That is—I'm afraid I can't have dinner with you this evening.'

5

'Why not?' Jordan was not a man to accept defeat so easily.

'Because—because I already have an appointment, as it happens,' she declared, justifying her words with a silent admonition to her conscience. After all, she had told Mrs Ingram she was going to make a start on clearing out the attic and despite the cold weather she had considered going up there tonight.

'I see.' She heard Jordan's impatient intake of breath. 'Tomorrow night, then.'

'I'm afraid not.'

'Another appointment?' His sarcasm was showing.

'No.' She moved the receiver to her other ear. 'As a matter of fact, I—I really don't want to have dinner with you, Jordan.'

'Afraid of making David jealous? From what I hear, I don't believe you have to worry on that score.'

'You swine, Jordan!'

'Oh, come.' He made an irritated sound. 'I don't want to row with you, Emma. I just want to talk to you, that's all. Nothing more.'

'No.'

She wanted to hang up on him then, but something kept her hanging on the line, despising herself for allowing him any opportunity to hurt her once again. Jordan Kyle was a past master in the art of hurting her, yet she still felt a tremor when she heard his voice.

'Emma . . .' He was obviously seeking for words. 'I have to talk to you. You could say it's—a matter of life and death.'

'Whose death?' Emma's mouth was dry. 'Yours?'

'Unfortunately not.' He paused. 'Well? Am I to be granted an audience?'

Emma hesitated. 'You—you could come to the house.

Have dinner with—with David and me, if you want to.'
But she crossed her fingers as she suggested this. David
would never sit down to a meal with Jordan Kyle.

Jordan sighed. 'No, Emma. That wouldn't do at all, and
you know it.'

'I'm sorry . . .'

'Are you?' He sounded sceptical. 'All right, Emma. If
I can't persuade you to change your mind . . . I'm sorry to
have troubled you.'

'Wait!' He was going to hang up on her. She knew it.
And at the same time, she couldn't allow it. 'I mean . . .' She
faltered as she tried to justify detaining him. 'Why did
you want to speak to me, Jordan?'

'You'll never know, will you?' he retorted equably, and
hung up on her.

Emma continued to sit there, holding the receiver, for
several agonising seconds. Then, as if it had suddenly
burned her, she replaced it on its rest, staring at it muti-
nously as the familiar resentment she felt towards Jordan
enveloped her in a wave of hot indignation. How dare he
ring her up like that? After all this time? How dare he
coolly invite her out to dinner when for the past eight
years he had apparently ignored her existence?

She drew a long steadying breath. Thank goodness she
had refused him, she thought, smoothing her hair with a
nervous gesture. At least she had shown him that he could
not drop her and then pick her up again when it suited him.
How she would have despised herself if she had given in to
his persuasions! And how David would have despised her
if he had found out!

Even so, her hands trembled as she reached for the
majolica vase she had been dusting when the telephone
rang. One had to admire his audacity, she thought reluctantly. No one could ever say that Jordan Kyle lacked

temerity. And there was no doubt, she was curious to know why he had suddenly chosen to contact her again. Could it have anything to do with the business? No. Her mother was no longer even a shareholder, and besides, if it had had to do with her mother's affairs, surely Jordan would have contacted her. But what else could it be? What other connection could there possibly be between the Kyle family and her own?

She was still standing by the desk, absently smoothing her duster over the cherubs' heads depicted on the vase, gazing blindly through the belling leaded panes of the shop window, when Gilda returned. The older woman came into the shop with its mellow chiming bell, closed the door and approached her assistant without Emma seeming to be aware of her. She stretched out a hand without speaking to rescue the fragile piece of pottery, and Emma's startled response was a justification for her employer's prudence.

'Oh, I'm sorry,' she gulped, as the vase fell harmlessly into Gilda's waiting hand. 'I—I was miles away.'

'So I noticed,' remarked Gilda dryly, setting the vase down safely on the desk. 'For heaven's sake, where were you? I was sure you hadn't heard the bell.'

'I hadn't.' Emma's face was flushed with embarrassment. 'You're back early. Did you get what you wanted?'

Gilda Avery removed the sheepskin jacket she was wearing over a slim-fitting jersey suit and hung it on the stand behind the desk. Then she held out her wrist watch for Emma to see.

'I don't know what time you think it is, my dear, but I make it a quarter to one. Don't you want any lunch today?'

'A quarter to one?' Emma could hardly believe it. What time had Jordan rung? Half past ten? Eleven? Whatever, she had been standing staring out of the window for well over an hour.

Shaking her head as if to shake away the sense of unreality which still gripped her, she exclaimed: 'I seem to have fallen asleep, don't I?' She forced a worried smile. 'I don't think I've missed any customers.'

'I'm sure you haven't,' drawled Gilda amiably, subsiding into her armchair and stretching her booted legs in front of her. 'God, I'm glad that's over. Dealing with someone on a one-to-one basis is always harder than outbidding buyers at an auction.'

'But did you get it?' Belatedly Emma was remembering the French *secretaire* Gilda had gone to see that morning, and realising that in her absence she had done next to nothing.

'Yes, I got it,' Gilda replied now, pulling out a pack of Gauloises and putting one between her lips. 'But ...' she lit the long French cigarette and inhaled deeply, '... at a vastly inflated price.'

'Then why didn't you——'

'—let it go?' Gilda shrugged her slim shoulders. 'I don't know. Perhaps I'm getting soft in my old age, or perhaps Lady Margaret was too persuasive.'

'I don't believe that.' Emma was striving for composure. 'I—I can tell by your face that it's what you wanted.'

'Oh, it is!' Gilda shed all pretence of indifference and enthusiasm shone in her light blue eyes. Drawing in her legs, she moved to the edge of her chair and resting her elbows on the desk, she exclaimed: 'Emma, it's exquisite. Really exquisite! It's a genuine Riesener, of course, and the marquetry is so intricate——' She broke off abruptly to draw on her cigarette again, looking up at her young assistant. 'You'll love it, Emma. It's so beautiful, I shan't want to sell it.'

Unable to sustain the penetration of those curiously intent blue eyes, Emma moved round the desk, her fingernail trailing lightly over its surface. 'Oh, I—I'm sure you will,' she murmured, forcing a light tone. 'Someone—some American—will come into the shop and offer you a fabulous price, and you'll be unable to resist.'

'Is that what you think?' Gilda continued to study the girl's unnaturally deepened colour. And then, with an abrupt change of topic, she said shrewdly: 'What's happened, Emma? Who's been here? Why are you so nervous suddenly? Did David call?'

'No.' At least that was true. Emma pushed back the heavy weight of her hair with a determined hand. 'You know what it's like when you've been day-dreaming and you're suddenly brought down to earth again. I—I guess I'm just a little off balance, that's all.'

Gilda's eyes narrowed. 'What were you day-dreaming about?'

'Oh, I don't know ...' Emma shrugged. 'This and that. Er—have you had lunch?'

'No. I'll have a sandwich here later.' She frowned. 'Emma, I don't want to probe, but if there's something worrying you, don't you think you should tell me? We've been friends a long time, and I've known your family for years. If there's something troubling you ...'

'Why should you think there's something troubling me?' Emma reached for her own suede coat and slipped her arms into the sleeves, and without waiting for an answer, added: 'What sort of sandwich do you want? Ham or cheese?'

'Ham, please.' Gilda rose to her feet. 'Emma, you're not having trouble with David again, are you? I mean—well, he's not being more objectionable than usual, is he?'

'No!' Emma pressed her lips together tightly. Then, as

if suddenly coming to a decision, she said shortly: 'It was Jordan. He rang.'

'Jordan Kyle!' Gilda's eyes widened disbelievingly.

'Do I know any other Jordan?' demanded Emma, with an attempt at levity. Then, tautly: 'Yes, of course. Jordan Kyle.'

Gilda breathed a sigh. 'Am I permitted to ask why he telephoned?'

'He asked me to have dinner with him.'

'He *what*?'

'Yes, I was surprised, too.' Emma shifted awkwardly. 'But there you are. The unexpected sometimes happens.'

'Yes.' Gilda regarded the girl opposite her with an anxious expression. 'And did you agree?'

'Heavens, no!' Emma was glad she could speak honestly. 'I told him I didn't want to have dinner with him. Besides,' she paused, 'David wouldn't approve, would he?'

'No,' Gilda agreed dryly. 'But then David isn't likely to approve of you doing anything that might upset his scheme of things.'

'Oh, Gilda!' Emma sighed. 'I know you don't like David. I know you have reason not to do so. But please, don't put me in the middle, like a bone between two dogs.'

Gilda shrugged. 'All right. Let's leave David, for the time being. Why did Jordan invite you to dinner?'

'He wouldn't tell me.'

'I see,' Gilda nodded. 'As enigmatic as usual. I wonder what's going on? Do you think he still finds you attractive?'

'Don't be silly!' Emma headed determinedly for the door. 'The only thing Jordan Kyle ever found attractive was Tryle Transmissions, and you know it.'

'Really?' Gilda resumed her seat. 'That's not what I heard.'

Unwillingly, Emma was intrigued. 'What—what do you mean?'

'Oh, nothing.' Gilda flicked over the pages of an inventory. 'Go get your lunch. And don't forget my sandwich. I'll have ham today.' She chuckled. 'I feel like a lion, not a mouse.'

'Gilda!' Emma clenched her fists, and as the woman looked up, she added: 'What do you know? What have you heard about Jordan? Is he involved with some girl? Is she married?'

'Does it matter to you?' Gilda's eyes softened. 'Oh, yes, I can see it does. Emma!' The tone was reproving now. 'I thought you'd got over all that foolishness.'

'I have.' Emma held up her head. 'But I've known Jordan all my life. Naturally I'm—interested in what happens to him.'

'All right.' Gilda picked up a pencil and toyed with it thoughtfully. 'He's been seen around with Stacey Albert. You know—her father has a controlling interest in——'

'—A.C.I. Yes, I know.' Emma nodded jerkily. 'The computer corporation.' She paused. 'Oh! Well, I didn't know that.' She cleared her throat. 'Are they—getting married?'

'Perhaps. Your Mr Kyle doesn't seem too eager to tie himself into that kind of situation, does he? I mean, he's what? Thirty-six? Thirty-seven? Quite old not to have been married already.'

The skin over Emma's cheekbones felt tight. 'Yes, well —like I said, the company was always his first and last love.'

'Maybe no longer,' observed Gilda wryly, but Emma reserved her opinion. Even so, the possibility of Jordan being involved with another woman still had the power to weaken her knees.

The antique shop stood in the High Street. Because Abingford's history dated back to feudal times, its size and reputation had spread, and in the season it was flooded with visitors from both sides of the Atlantic. Its timbered buildings were world-famous, and its cathedral dreamed beside the placid waters of the River Avon. It was near enough to Stratford, and the other attractions of the Cotswolds, to merit half a dozen decent hotels, but it still maintained the atmosphere of the country town it had always been. It was far enough from London not to attract a commuter population, yet near enough for a day's visit using the efficient rail link. Emma had lived there all her life—at least, apart from the two years she had lived in London; and her family had lived in the district for as long as she could remember.

Today, as she hurried along the High Street and turned into Hunter's Mews, however, she was paying little attention to her surroundings. Not even the east wind, bringing with it little flurries of snow, could distract her from the chaotic turmoil of her thoughts, and she had passed the butcher's shop before she realised she needed to call in there. Turning back, she bought the fillet steak David liked grilled to a juicy rareness, and then hastened on towards Mellor Terrace.

Before Emma and David were married, David's mother had lived in the house in this pleasant Georgian terrace, but when the wedding was planned, she had insisted on finding a flat and giving the house to her son as a wedding gift. In consequence, its furnishings were rather old-fashioned, with lots of dark furniture in rooms that were themselves inclined to be gloomy. Emma had planned to change all that. She and David had discussed interior decorating and colour schemes in those few short weeks of their engagement, but afterwards—after disaster had struck—he had lost all interest in changing anything. On the contrary, he seemed to cling to those things that were familiar with an almost obsessive grasp, and the idea of going against his wishes was unthinkable. Even so, there were times when Emma felt her mother-in-law's hand in the matter, and guessed that Mrs Ingram was using David's disability to her own advantage. She had always been a possessive woman, and the abnormality of their marriage made her position that much stronger.

Letting herself into the house in Mellor Terrace, Emma immediately sensed the presence of the only other person who had a key to her home. It was an intangible awareness compounded of their mutual antipathy, and the more physical evidence of her mother-in-law's slightly cloying perfume. Attar of roses drifted along the hall, and with it the murmured sound of voices.

Emma was removing her coat when the wheels of David's chair heralded his emergence from the living room. His hands on the wheels brought the chair to an abrupt halt when he saw her, and his pale features assumed the somewhat peevish air he invariably adopted with her these days.

'You're late,' he observed shortly. 'Fortunately, Mother's here to keep me company, or I should have been most concerned. Doesn't Gilda Avery know that I expect you home at a quarter past twelve?'

Sighing, Emma went to bestow a kiss on his cheek. 'I'm sorry, darling,' she murmured apologetically, ignoring the impulse to defend herself. 'Gilda had an important meeting this morning, and I had to hold the fort until she got back.'

'If you ask me, I think that woman detains you deliberately,' remarked Mrs Ingram, coming out of the living room to stand behind her son. A tall, well-built woman, she tended to overpower any opposition, but Emma had had plenty of experience in defying her.

'Gilda wouldn't do that,' she said now, smiling in the face of hostility, knowing full well that Mrs Ingram would prefer her to argue, thus giving her an opportunity to gain her son's support.

'I don't know why you have to work anyway,' added her mother-in-law, digging up an old bone of contention. 'Heaven knows, David spends enough time on his own as it is. I can't imagine why you persistently follow your own career at the expense of your husband's happiness.'

Emma's tongue probed her upper lip. Then she said firmly: 'David understands. I need an occupation. And so far as being alone is concerned, David wouldn't want me around all the time. When he's working——'

'*When* I'm working,' put in David moodily. 'A rare and wonderful occurrence these days.'

'Oh, David . . .'

Whenever he got on about the shortage of commissions coming his way these days, Emma felt guilty. And yet his work was as good as ever. His artistic talents had not been impaired at all, but his attitude of mind coloured his illustrations, and his London agent had confided that unless David could shed his almost manic preoccupation with misery and suffering he would no longer be able to represent him. It was just an added problem to the already overloaded problem of their lives, and there were times when Emma wished it could have been she who had been crippled in the crash. It was at times like these when she chided herself for insisting on continuing with her job, but most of the time she accepted that without the three days a week she spent at Avery Antiques she would go mad.

Now, leaving David to offer his mother another glass of sherry, she went into the kitchen and turned on the grill. The steaks would not take long, and as she had bought extra to go into the freezer it was no problem to cater for three instead of two. Mrs Ingram was a frequent visitor to the house, and Emma had long abandoned the idea of being mistress in her own home.

Lunch was ready in half an hour, and seated at the square mahogany table in the dining room overlooking the walled garden at the back of the house, Emma relaxed a little. Why not? she asked herself, sipping at the glass of wine David had produced to drink with the meal. It was perfectly natural that hearing from Jordan again after all this time should have disconcerted her, but she was over the worst now and she was glad she had confided in Gilda. She was the only person she could confide in, and telling her had lessened the impact somehow. All the same, there was still the element of unease in not knowing what he had wanted, but that would dissipate with time. He had probably been at a loose end, she thought wryly. He must have been, to ring her when he had made it brutally plain in the past that their relationship had meant nothing serious to him. Did he think perhaps that now she was married she might be more accommodating? What kind of relationship did he think she had with David? Or didn't he think about David at all?

Yet, if what Gilda said was true, he already had an accommodating girl-friend. Stacey Albert was a very sophisticated young lady, so why was Jordan bothering with the girl he had once known and discarded, the girl he had shed like an unwanted toy when her father sank into debt and finally killed himself? Her lips tightened. Oh, yes, as soon as the firm of Trace and Kyle, known familiarly as Tryle Transmissions, was bought out by the Kyle family, he no longer made any pretence of his feelings towards his father's partner's daughter.

'Do you have to go back to the shop this afternoon?'

Mrs Ingram was speaking to her, and Emma looked up

half guiltily, as if afraid her thoughts were visible for everyone to read.

'I—beg your pardon? What? Oh, yes. Yes. I promised Gilda I'd take her a sandwich. She's had no lunch.'

'Can't she afford to buy her own sandwiches?' demanded David testily, pouring more wine into his glass. 'You aren't paid to feed your employer as well as yourself, are you?'

'No,' agreed Emma, biting her tongue on the desire to tell him that without her salary they couldn't afford to drink wine at lunchtime either, and Mrs Ingram took up the comment.

'She really is the most objectionable woman,' she declared, with a sniff. 'When I asked her to contribute to our charity fund, she had the nerve to tell me that her taxes alone would feed and clothe half the population of Abingford and she didn't see why she should contribute when the state had millions of pounds just waiting to be applied for.'

Emma hid a smile. 'Well, that is true,' she conceded quietly. 'People simply won't claim, and Gilda says she doesn't see why she should give money to organisations who spend half of it to pay the administratory costs.'

Mrs Ingram's head went up. 'I hope you're not implying, Emma, that my colleagues in the Ladies' Guild and I use the money we collect for any other purpose than that for which it's intended.'

'Oh, no.' Emma shook her head, assuming an innocent expression. 'I'm only telling you what Gilda thinks.'

'Huh!' Mrs Ingram attacked her steak with more vigour. 'As I said before, she's an objectionable woman, and I can't imagine why David permits you to work for her.'

'Why David permits ...' Emma was almost driven into retaliation, but just in time she bit back the words. 'I just do a job, Mrs Ingram,' she declared evenly. 'Now, do you want cheesecake or crackers, David?'

To her relief, the topic was dropped, but when she left for the shop later she was aware that her mother-in-law had not given up on it. No doubt she would use this time alone with David to pursue her point, and Emma could only hope that, as in the past, Mrs Ingram would over-reach herself. David could be as perverse as his mother, and if he suspected he was being manipulated, he would retaliate in kind. It had happened before, and both Emma and his mother knew what a precarious game they were playing.

Gilda was busy with a customer when Emma re-entered the antique shop a few minutes later. They were studying a catalogue of Italian ceramics, and Emma removed her coat and picked up her duster to complete the tidying of the shelves she had begun before Jordan's phone call. She was admiring a display of Victorian miniatures when the door-bell chimed once more, and she turned smilingly to deal with the new customer. But the smile was frozen on her face as she recognised the newcomer. It might be some time since she had seen Jordan Kyle in the flesh, but he was sufficiently newsworthy to warrant the occasional write-up in the local press and because of this she had not been allowed to forget his lean features.

Now, coming face to face with him, she was struck anew by the magnetism he exercised, the powerful influence that had once wrought such havoc in her life. Tall, around six feet, she estimated, with a strong if leanly built body, he looked more like an athlete than a businessman. His legs were long and muscular, and he moved with a litheness that belied his thirty-seven years. He was not handsome, but Emma had long since come to the conclusion that handsome men were rarely attractive to women. Jordan Kyle's harsh, uncompromising features—the deep-set, hooded eyes, the high cheekbones and roughly set nose, the thin line of his mouth—combined to give his face a hard, almost cruel disposition, and yet when he smiled and displayed uneven white teeth, he had a fascination that was impossible to ignore. And to complete his appearance, his hair was that peculiar shade known as ash-blond, which meant it could look silver in some lights. He wore it short on top, but it grew low down the base of his neck, and Emma knew from experience it was strong and vital to the touch.

All these things were evident to her in those first few seconds when her blood ran cold in her veins and burned like a banner in her cheeks. Jordan Kyle. Coming to see her after all this time. The last she had heard about him, he had been spending several weeks with his father who had lately retired to live in the West Indies, and his tan which looked so unusual against the lightness of his hair was further evidence that the English winter had meant little to him.

'Hello, Emma,' he said now, closing the door behind him with a little click. His words attracted Gilda's attention, and for a brief moment they, too, exchanged glances, then her customer demanded attention and Jordan transferred all his attention to her assistant.

Clearing her throat, Emma managed not to let her smile disappear completely. It was four years since she had actually spoken to Jordan, and then only in passing at a charity ball organised by David's mother. He had been with someone else then, a girl she couldn't even remember. All she could remember was going to the ladies' room and spending fifteen minutes in the toilet gaining control of herself again.

'Hello, Jordan,' she responded now, folding her duster meticulously between her fingers. Tightening her lips, she added, in what she hoped was a casual tone: 'I didn't know you were interested in antiques.'

'I'm not.' Jordan glanced round the cluttered shop with faint contempt. Then he looked at Emma again. 'You know why I'm here. Is there somewhere we can talk?'

'This is the showroom,' replied Emma tautly. 'Whatever you have to say, it can be said here.'

'No, it can't,' he contradicted, looking beyond her to the door leading into the tiny office at the back of the shop. 'Can we go in there?' He gestured towards the office. 'What I have to say is for your ears alone.'

'How mysterious!' Emma tried to be facetious, but it didn't quite come off. Looking doubtfully at Gilda, she murmured in a low voice: 'Was it necessary to come to the shop? Why couldn't you have told me over the telephone?'

Jordan's sigh was irritable. 'Look, Emma, I don't have all day. Are you going to speak to me or aren't you?'

She licked her dry lips. 'And if I say no?'

'I'll leave,' he stated grimly, and she knew he would.

'But what can you have to say that—that's so important?' she exclaimed. Then, viewing his uncompromising features, she capitulated. 'Oh, very well. Come in here.'

Ignoring Gilda's speculative stare, she led the way into the tiny office at the back which was as cluttered in its way as the shop. Jordan looked about him impatiently as he closed the door, and in the small office his presence was that much more disturbing.

'My God,' he said, as she moved round the desk to put it as a physical barrier between them. 'How do you find anything in this place?'

'I imagine we manage,' she replied, gripping the edge of the desk tightly for support. 'Now, do you mind telling me why you're here?'

'Well, as you refused to eat a meal with me, I had no other alternative,' he responded, and his dark eyes which were such a contrast to the lightness of his hair were suddenly compelling. 'I wanted to talk to you—to ask your assistance—and I couldn't do that over a telephone.'

'To—ask my assistance!' Emma sat down rather suddenly, as her legs gave out on her. 'You want *my* assistance?' She shook her head. 'How can I help you?'

Jordan came to the desk and leant upon it, his long-fingered hands, the only artistic thing about him, spread squarely on the polished surface. His nails were always clean, she thought inconsequently, mesmerised by his closeness, by the clean male smell of him emanating from the opened buttons of his black leather car coat. But she dared not look up at him, and her eyes became glued somewhere between the waistband of his pants and the swinging pendulum of his tie.

'My father is dying,' he said, without preamble. 'He wants to see you. He wants to see *us*—reconciled, for want of a better word.'

CHAPTER TWO

EMMA was glad she was sitting down. His words delivered in that curt uncompromising manner were completely emotionless, but that didn't prevent them from shocking her to the core of her being. Andrew Kyle was dying! The man who had once been like a second father to her had only a limited time to live. She found it impossible to accept.

'But—what's——'

'Cancer,' retorted Jordan coldly. 'It's terminal. The doctors gave him approximately six months.'

'Does—does he know?'

'I believe so.' He straightened. 'He's not a fool. He knows the score. I imagine that's why he wants to—put his affairs in order.'

'But—but why me?' Emma gazed up at him with troubled eyes. 'I—he hasn't seen me for—oh, seven or eight years. Not since—not since you took over the company, in fact.'

'I know that.' Jordan thrust his hands deep into the pockets of his coat. 'But now he wants to see you, and I'm here to find out how you feel about it.'

'How I feel about it.'

Emma shook her head. How *did* she feel about it? Naturally, she pitied anyone served that kind of death sentence, but how could she be expected to feel any kind of personal involvement for so long she had forced herself not to think about the Kyles, father and son? And why should he want to see her anyway? He had shown no obvious distress when she and Jordan went their separate ways, and to receive this summons now was like opening up an old wound.

'Well?'

Jordan was regarding her intently and she shifted awkwardly beneath that penetrating gaze. What was he thinking? she wondered. Did he resent having to come here and ask her for anything? Or was he perhaps comparing her to the woman he had known, and finding her wanting? Certainly, her straight rope of glossy dark hair could not compare to the champagne brilliance of Stacey Albert's silken curls, and apart from her eyes, which were a mixture of violet and blue and set between long curling lashes, her features were quite ordinary. She was tall, of course, which was an advantage, but not willowy enough by today's yardsticks. Her breasts were far too prominent, and although her legs were slim, her hips were not.

Now she rose to her feet again, and feeling at less of a disadvantage said: 'Tell me where your father is, and I'll go and see him.'

'You will?' Jordan's features relaxed somewhat. 'Thank you.'

'That's all right.' Emma held up her head. 'Uncle—that is, your father—was always very kind to me. And I know —I know Daddy would want me to do as you ask, despite —despite everything.'

Jordan bent his head thoughtfully, and as the silence between them stretched, Emma spoke again.

'How—how is your mother taking this?'

'My mother?' Jordan looked up in surprise. 'Didn't you know? My mother is dead. She died eighteen months ago.'

'I'm sorry.' Emma was aghast at her mistake. 'I—I didn't know. No one ever said ...'

'Why should they?' Jordan seemed unmoved, and she

flinched from his hard indifference. 'It was a long way away, and the press are really only interested if they can get an angle on a story. If there's something unusual or scandalous to write about. My mother's death would make dull reading.'

Emma pressed her lips together and looked down at the desk. Then she said quietly: 'Just tell me where your father is staying, and I'll make arrangements to see him as soon as possible.'

'Ah, yes.' Jordan's mocking tone brought her head up again. 'Well, that's where we run into a slight problem.'

'A slight problem? What do you mean?' Emma frowned.

'My father lives on an island in the Caribbean. Didn't you know that either?'

Emma gasped. 'Well, yes—yes, I knew that. But I naturally assumed . . .'

'What did you assume? That he'd come to England to die?' Jordan shook his head. 'Oh, no. Nothing would persuade my father to come back to this country now, particularly not in the middle of winter. No, Valentia is his home, and that's where he'll die.'

'But—but what about his treatment?'

'What treatment? He's had two operations, and various radiation therapy. He knows there's nothing more anyone can do for him, except prevent him from suffering any more pain than is absolutely necessary.'

'Oh, Jordan!'

The helpless words fell from her lips, and for a brief moment she saw the spasm of pain that crossed his face. But then it was gone again, and she was left with the impression that perhaps she had imagined it.

'So . . .' He flexed his shoulder muscles. 'Does this make a difference to the situation?'

'You must know it does.' Emma shifted her weight restlessly from one foot to the other. 'I mean—how can I go out to the West Indies? I have a home—and a husband.' She avoided his eyes as she said this. 'I can't just abandon them without thought or consideration.'

'No one's asking you to,' replied Jordan shortly. 'I realise how difficult it would be for you. And I'm quite prepared to accept your refusal, should you feel you can't do it.'

Emma expelled her breath on a heavy sigh. Then she faced him squarely. 'You don't really care, do you?' she exclaimed tautly. 'You don't really want me to go out there.'

'If I've given that impression, then I'm sorry,' replied Jordan politely. 'Naturally I want what's best for my father. And if he wants to see you, I shall do everything in my power to accommodate him.'

'To accommodate him?' Emma's lips trembled at the dispassionate tone of his voice. 'You're so cold, aren't you, Jordan? So unfeeling. To you it's just another job of work, and if anyone's feelings are hurt, then hard luck!'

'I see no reason for you to feel so emotively about it,' he retorted harshly. 'As you've already pointed out, my father has ignored your existence for several years. Why should you rush to his defence now?'

'He's dying, Jordan.'

'And does that eradicate the sins of the past? Are you one of those people who believes that repentance equals forgiveness?'

'What are you saying, Jordan? What sin has your father committed? Ignoring my existence hardly warrants condemnation.'

'In your eyes, perhaps not,' he conceded stiffly. 'Very well. Do I take it that you'll come?'

Emma turned her back on him, resting her chin on her knuckles, trying desperately to decide what she ought to do. Obviously, she could make no decision without first discussing it with David, and she already knew what his reaction would be. But here and now she had to decide whether she wanted to go, whether there was any point in holding out hope that she would agree.

After a few moments, she said: 'What—what would be the arrangements? How would I get to—to Valentia?'

There was a pause, and then Jordan replied: 'A direct flight operates between London and Barbados. An inter-island transport flies between Seawell and Valentia.'

'I see.' Emma turned again, slowly. 'And—and how long would all this take? I mean—how long would I be away?'

Jordan shrugged. 'That would be up to you, of course. Technically, the flight to Barbados takes something like ten hours, but bearing in mind the four-hour time lag, you can complete the journey in half a day. The inter-island flight is much shorter—a matter of forty minutes, no more.'

'And—flights to Valentia; they're pretty frequent?'

'No.' Jordan shook his head. 'Generally they're laid on when required. Valentia's population doesn't exceed five hundred, so as you can imagine, there's not a lot of need for a regular service.'

Emma absorbed this with difficulty. Somehow she couldn't imagine herself flying off to the West Indies at a moment's notice, going to see a man to whom she was practically a stranger, seeing sights and people totally alien to her normally limited existence. She had seen pictures of the Caribbean islands, shared a common longing for their beauty and tranquillity. But never at any time had she seriously considered going there. She wasn't at all sure she wanted the dream exposing, for nothing was ever quite as attractive as one anticipated.

'I'll have to talk it over with David,' she said at last, and Jordan's lean mouth turned downward at the corners.

'Then you might as well give me your answer right now,'

he remarked cynically. 'We both know Ingram will never agree to your going anywhere with me.'

'With—with you?' Emma's eyes were wide.

'Why, yes, with me,' agreed Jordan dryly. 'You didn't imagine I would let you fly out there on your own, did you?'

Emma made a helpless gesture. 'I thought—that is—the company——'

'I have a very capable general manager,' Jordan interrupted her curtly. 'Even I am not so heartless as to let my father die alone. At the moment, I'm dividing my time between Abingford and Valentia, but as the time runs out, I'll stay on the island.' His lips twisted. 'There are telephones. My father saw to that.'

Emma didn't know what to say. Considering going to Valentia alone was one thing. Contemplating the trip with the one man she had hoped never to see again was quite another.

'I need some time,' she said now, pushing back her hair with a nervous hand. 'Surely you can grant me a couple of days. When are you leaving?'

'At the end of next week,' he answered, taking his hands out of his pockets to fasten his coat. 'When will you let me know what you've decided? At the weekend? Or is that too soon?'

'No—no.' That gave her three days. 'No, I'll know by the weekend.'

'Good. Will you ring me?'

Emma linked her fingers together. 'I don't have your number.'

'It hasn't changed,' he reminded her shortly. 'Abingford double-six-one-nine. Or you can ring me at the office. I'm sure you remember that number.'

Emma's skin prickled. 'My father's number, you mean?'

she countered tautly, and saw the faint colour run up under his tan.

'You remember,' he observed, and turning, opened the door into the showroom. 'Until the weekend, then ...'

Emma nodded, and followed him out into the now empty shop, empty, that was, but for Gilda lounging carelessly on the edge of her desk. When she saw them, her eyes flickered thoughtfully, then she put aside the pen she had been holding and smiled.

'Good afternoon, Jordan,' she said, the mockery in her tones only lightly veiled. 'This is an unexpected honour.'

Jordan's expression was equally sardonic. 'Good afternoon, Gilda,' he responded in kind. 'Still as defensive as ever, I see.'

'Defensive!' Gilda straightened to face him, and then subsided again as she realised she was automatically proving his point. Controlling her temper, she said: 'Might one ask why you're slumming? I'm sure you have enough antiques in that mansion of yours to furnish half a dozen salerooms, so I can't believe that's why you're here.'

Jordan smiled then, and Emma had to admire his self-control. 'You're right, of course, Gilda,' he agreed imperturbably, turning up the collar of his coat against the cold outside. 'Quite enough antiques. Yes. Nice to have seen you again. G'bye, Emma!' And with a polite nod to both of them he left.

'Conceited bastard!' declared Gilda as soon as the door had closed behind him, and Emma was glad of the brief respite to collect her own composure. 'What did he want? Can't he take no for an answer? You did say you had refused his invitation, didn't you?'

'Yes, of course.' Emma turned aside to rescue the sandwich she had brought for her employer from her handbag. 'Here you are: ham! Are you ravenous?'

'Not particularly, but put the kettle on, will you?' said Gilda, peeling the sealing plastic from the roll. Then, as Emma moved to comply, she added: 'Well? Are you going to tell me what he wanted, or aren't you?'

Emma sighed. 'His father wants to see me, that's all.'

'Old Andrew?'

'Not so old. He must be about—sixty-five.'

'Even so ...' Gilda was perplexed. 'I didn't know he'd come back to live at Athelmere.'

'He hasn't.'

Emma disappeared into the back office to fill the kettle in the tiny cloakroom adjoining, but Gilda moved to stand, eating her sandwich, at the open doorway, and she was waiting for her when she emerged again.

'Emma ...' she said, chewing almost absently. 'Emma, he hasn't asked you to go out to the Caribbean, has he?'

'As a matter of fact——'

'But why? Emma, why?' She gulped. 'You can be considering it!'

Emma plugged in the kettle. 'Why not?'

'Why? Why, because—because—how do you know it's his father who wants to see you? How do you know it's not some devious——'

'Gilda!' Emma's impatient use of her name silenced her. 'Don't be foolish! Jordan Kyle isn't interested in me. Good heavens, you said yourself he was involved with Stacey Albert! And in any case, aren't you forgetting—I'm married!'

'Is that what you call it?' retorted Gilda sharply. 'Being at the beck and call of a man who's only half a man!'

'*Gilda!*' Emma was trembling now as much with nervous reaction as indignation, although she would never have admitted it. 'Gilda, David isn't responsible for his condition.'

'Isn't he?' Gilda was unsympathetic. 'Who is, then? Who

else was at the wheel of the car if it wasn't himself? He was
alone when they found him, wasn't he? You can't blame
yourself for that.'

'I don't. I just wish you wouldn't talk like that about—
about my husband.'

'But he's not your husband, is he?' pursued Gilda relent-
lessly. 'He never has been. And don't forget, I was with you
that week before the wedding. I know the doubts you had,
long before Master Ingram chose to smash himself, and your
relationship, before it had even been consummated.'

'Oh, Gilda . . .' Emma dropped two teabags into the pot.
'Must you keep bringing that up? David and I are married.
We've been married for almost four years. Why can't you
accept it? There's no point in thinking about what might
have been. This is here and now, and there's no—no——'

'Escape?' suggested Gilda dryly, but Emma vigorously
denied it.

'No. I was about to say there's no—altering it. That's
all.'

'All right.' Gilda finished the sandwich and delicately
licked her fingers. 'So where does that leave us? Oh, yes—
Jordan's invitation to temptation.'

'Gilda!' The kettle boiled at that moment, and she made
the tea with hands that spattered drops of boiling water all
over the papers on the desk. 'Jordan's father is ill. He wants
to see me before—in case—anything happens.'

'I see,' Gilda nodded.

'That's confidential, Gilda.'

'Of course,' Gilda agreed. 'But that doesn't answer the
question, does it? Are you seriously considering going?'

'I don't know . . .' Emma added milk to the teacups. 'I
honestly don't know.'

The chiming of the shop bell brought their conversation
to an abrupt halt, and leaving Gilda to drink her tea in

peace, Emma went to attend to the customer. For the rest of the afternoon, she was kept busy and although she knew that Gilda only had her well-being at heart, she was relieved. The whole situation was too new, too fraught with difficulties, to discuss coherently, and the arrival of Gilda's latest boy-friend just before closing time curtailed any prolonged farewells.

'See you Friday,' she called, as she left the shop, but she was not unaware of her employer's impatience at the knowledge that it would be two days before she heard her decision.

Outside, Frank Horner's Jaguar was parked at the kerb. A man in his early fifties, he had already been married twice before, and Gilda was his present quarry. Gilda herself took him much less seriously. She had not reached the age of forty-two without learning a little about the opposite sex, and while her slim figure and good looks attracted plenty of attention, she seldom got seriously involved with anyone. She was a career woman, first and foremost, and the income from the shop more than compensated any need for security. Emma doubted she would ever get married, despite Frank Horner's ambitions.

David's mother had left by the time she got home, and to her relief David was engrossed in his study, working on his present commission. He spared a moment to greet her, and then, while she set the casserole she had prepared at lunchtime on a low light and went to bathe and change before serving their evening meal, he returned to his work.

Later, eating their meal from a serving trolley set before the fire in the drawing room, Emma let herself relax. It was pleasant in the lamplit room with the television playing away quietly in one corner, there to be seen or not as the mood took her. She could almost convince herself that they were any ordinary couple sitting eating their supper together, until David got bored with quiet domesticity and thrust his tray savagely aside.

'God, I wish this weather would improve!' he muttered, reaching for the bottle of Scotch on the table beside him and splashing a generous measure into his glass. 'I'm so sick of being confined to this house, day in and day out! I get so bored I could scream!'

Emma gathered the dirty dishes together on to the trolley. 'We could go out tomorrow, if you like,' she offered mildly, looking up to see his reaction, and predictably, he scowled.

'With you driving?' he demanded, and then shook his head. 'You know I hate being driven by a woman.'

'I know that. But unless you do——'

'I know, I know. Don't remind me. Unless you drive, I can't go anywhere.'

'David, you know you could have transport ...'

'One of those ghastly three-wheelers? No, thanks!'

'No. I believe there are other vehicles——'

'It doesn't matter. They're all the same. They all have *disabled driver* on the back.'

'Well, that's what you are, David,' Emma pointed out quietly. 'Surely you see that if you could only accept that, things would be so much easier ...'

'For you, you mean. Would it take some of the guilt from your shoulders knowing I was mobile?'

Emma sighed. They had had this argument before and it always ended the same. 'David, accepting your disability would make it easier for you, too. Don't you see? There's so much in life to enjoy——'

'Not in my life. I'm just a living vegetable. I just about manage to feed and clothe myself, and that's all.'

'You have your work ...'

'My work!' David snorted. 'Do you think I don't know that all the jobs I get now are second-rate commissions?

Langley never sends me anything worthwhile any more. That's why he never comes here. He daren't show his face.'

'David, Harry Langley doesn't come here because you're so unpleasant to him when he does, that's all. And I think you're wrong. The commissions he sends you are good commissions. It's just that you don't take the—the interest in them that you used to do.'

'Don't give me that! I'm interested all right. David Ingram used to be a name to be reckoned with, and I'm not about to give that up.'

'Then—then stop feeling so sorry for yourself!' exclaimed Emma urgently. 'And stop drinking so much. That's the second bottle of Scotch you've started this week.'

'Who's counting?' retorted David, and deliberately refilled his glass.

Shaking her head, Emma rose and wheeled the trolley out of the room. It was useless trying to reason with him, particularly when he'd been drinking. His self-pity was absolute, and she could see no end to it.

As she loaded the dishes into the sink, she pondered the improbabilities of her life thus far. Gilda had been accurate about the doubts she had had before her marriage to David. There had been times in those weeks before the wedding when she had considered calling the whole thing off. She had not loved David as she should have done, but he had known that and wanted her anyway, and she had foolishly allowed herself to be persuaded.

It was all down to her feelings for Jordan Kyle. Maybe if she had never known him, her affection for David would have been enough. As it was, she had known what love could be like between a man and a woman, and didn't they always say that a woman never forgot her first affair?

She sighed, dipping her hands into the soapy water. The trouble was, she had never known a time when Jordan had not played some part in her life. She remembered when she was little more than a toddler and he was already twelve or thirteen years old, the way he had given her rides on his back, taught her how to swim, had snowball fights with her, and given her trips on the crossbar of his bicycle. As she grew older he was always there, to tease or mock, to chide or admire, the older brother she had never known. Because they were both only children, and because their fathers were partners in business, it was natural that they should see a lot of one another, and by the time Emma was eighteen and home from boarding school, her infatuation for Jordan was complete.

The magical thing had been that he appeared to feel the same. For all there were ten years between them, he had never seriously bothered with any other girl, and that summer of her maturity had been the most marvellous summer of her life. Although even then Jordan had already joined the company and was starting to make a name for himself in the cold hard world of finance, all his free time he had spent with Emma, and their relationship became the most important thing in her life. She had adored him with all the stirring passion of her youth, and had been able to deny him nothing ...

The blade of a knife skimmed her finger, and a thread of blood appeared along the parting skin. With an exclamation, she ran the cut under cold water, wondering whether the careless gesture had been an omen. Certainly it epitomised the savagery of their parting when it happened; she had felt then that she was bleeding—but inside.

It had happened so suddenly, so unexpectedly, so *brutally*. So wrapped up in her own feelings had she been, she had not noticed the strain in her father's face which had increased daily, the anxiety her mother must have been feeling. Instead, when the crash came, it tore into her like a

physical blast, shattering her home and her family, everything she had held dear.

Her mother had stood up well under the strain. She had
blamed Emma's father entirely, and perhaps this had been
her means of recovery. And it was true, Jeremy Trace had
been gambling recklessly, using shareholders' money to
subsidise his debts. He had always enjoyed the good life,
sometimes to the detriment of his wife and daughter, but
inevitably time had caught up with him. Even then, he had
taken the easiest way out. He had shot himself in the library
of their home, leaving his womenfolk to settle his debts and
face the inevitable scandal that followed.

Andrew Kyle had tried to help them, but naturally he
had to think of his shareholders first, and in any case, her
mother had not wanted his assistance. Instead, she had sold
the house standing adjacent to the Kyle home, and moved
herself and Emma into a tiny flat in Abingford, overlooking
the yard of St Stephen's Church.

During this traumatic time, Emma had seen little of
Jordan, or his parents. She had not thought a lot about it,
being in the grip of her own grief, and needing to comfort
her mother. But as the weeks passed and the scandal died
down, he still continued to avoid her, and her suspicions
were born.

It took some time before the truth gradually began to sink
in. Jordan had been interested in her only so long as she
was her father's daughter. By marrying her, he would
have gained ultimate control of both family's shareholdings.
Once that situation no longer applied, he had decided to cut
his losses. Why marry a girl without a penny to her name
when there were plenty of well-heeled ladies around only
too willing to share their inheritance with a man as attractive as Jordan Kyle?

She had considered the possibility that perhaps her

father's suicide and the scandal which had ensued might have affected his feelings towards her, but she couldn't believe Jordan to be so small-minded, so the obvious explanation seemed the most probable.

Whatever, Emma had suffered a severe relapse herself. Her relationship with Jordan had been such that she had never given the idea of not marrying him any serious consideration, and to discover that he had deceived her in that way had been more than she could bear. As soon as she was capable of finding a job, she had taken herself off to London, wanting to put as much distance between herself and the Kyles as was humanly possible. Her mother had encouraged her decision, and Emma had decided that so far as her mother was concerned, the break-up of their relationship had not been unexpected.

Inevitably, time wrought its own miracles of healing. Emma was lucky enough to get a job in an auction house in London. She had always been interested in antiques, and her apprenticeship there served her in good stead when she finally returned to Abingford. She came back when she discovered her mother was finding it difficult to live on the allowance she made her, and for a while Emma shared the flat with her again.

It was about this time she met David Ingram once more.

She had met him first in Jordan's company. David was a freelance commercial artist, working at that time on an advertising campaign for Tryle Transmissions. She had known immediately that she attracted him, but whether that was because she was the boss's girl-friend or not, she could never be sure. What had always been apparent was that any girl who could hold a man like Jordan had to have something, and several of his friends had made passes at her when they thought Jordan wasn't looking.

Emma had quite liked David, although she had sensed

his feelings towards Jordan contained quite an element of envy. He had always had an intense ambition to be wealthy, and having money meant a lot to him.

From the minute he learned that Emma was back in Abingford to stay, he had started dating her, and within a very short time he asked her to marry him. Emma had demurred, insisting that they hardly knew one another, secretly wondering whether Jordan might ring her once he knew she was home again. She knew he was still unmarried, unattached, if what the papers said was true, and she cherished hopes that perhaps time would have worked its miracle for him, too.

But as the weeks and months went by, and there was no word from Jordan, she was forced to accept that so far as he was concerned, their affair was over. Her mother, guessing her feelings, had ridiculed such foolishness. David, she said, was a far better candidate than Jordan Kyle could ever be, and besides, she wanted Emma to have nothing more to do with that family.

The crunch came the night Emma casually encountered Jordan at the charity ball. He had spoken to her politely, but that was all. His eyes had looked straight through her and she had known that whatever there had been between them was dead—and buried. That was the night she had accepted David's proposal, and lived to regret it. His accident, just four days before the date of the wedding, had destroyed any idea she might have had for cancelling the ceremony. Instead, it had been conducted around his bed in the hospital, the only thing, they said, that would give him a reason for living. *A reason for living* ...

Emma pressed her lips together tightly now. That was ironic. From the moment David learned that he was paralysed from the waist down, he had despised the life he was forced to live, and gradually he was forcing Emma to despise

her life, too. It was as if there was a malignant cancer growing inside him that was gradually corrupting his soul, and
Emma seldom looked into the future without a sense of
despair.

If only David had accepted his disability. If only he
could appreciate how good it was to be alive, instead of
persistently bemoaning his lot in life, and allowing the envy
he had always possessed to poison and destroy what little
happiness they might have had.

'Emma!' She heard him calling her now, the irritability
evident in his voice. 'Emma, what in God's name are you
doing? Does it take half an hour to make a cup of coffee?'

'*Coffee!*' Emma started guiltily. She had forgotten to
turn on the percolator.

'I won't be long,' she called in reply. 'I'm just finishing
the dishes!' and as if to emphasise this point she clattered
plates and dishes on to the draining board.

But later that night, lying in the lonely isolation of her
bed, she gave in to the frustrated tears that stung the backs
of her eyes. She and David didn't even share a bedroom,
he having decided he needed the double bed they had once
intended to use for his own use downstairs, while she
occupied the single divan in the bedroom upstairs. How
could she suggest going to the West Indies? she thought
helplessly. Apart from anything else, it was unfair to David
to even think of such a thing when he was stuck here at
home, hating the cold weather. There had never been
money for expensive holidays. Even the accident insurance
had been denied to them on a technicality, which Emma had
never understood, and without her job in those early days
they would have had to have applied for social security.

Besides, what could Andrew Kyle have to say to her that
was so desperately important that he should send for her
practically on his dying bed? It didn't make sense to her,

so how could David be expected to understand, let alone agree to the trip?

She sighed. Jordan would not be surprised if she refused. Relieved, was his more likely reaction. After all, how boring it would be for him having to escort her all that way, and embarrassing, too, if she chose to bring up the past. But she wouldn't do that, she thought, fumbling under her pillow for a paper tissue. She had some pride! Of course, he didn't know that, and now he would never find out.

CHAPTER THREE

THE attic at Mellor Terrace was dark and gloomy, the only light coming through a tiny window set up high in the roof. There was no electricity, and Emma had to use a torch to see what she was doing. It was chilly, too, but she had put on thick trousers and a chunky sweater, and the effort of her exertions was keeping the cold at bay.

Looking round the cobwebby interior of the attic, she wondered how many years it was since anyone had been up here. Mrs Ingram had shuddered at the prospect of climbing the rickety old staircase that coiled to the upper regions of the house, and she had shown little interest in Emma's plans to clean the place out. One of her arguments for Emma giving up her job was to imply that she had not the time to keep up with her housework, but she ignored the fact that she had not entered the attic so long as Emma had known her.

David had been much less emphatic. On the contrary, he had stated that as there was never likely to be more than two of them living in the house, the three spare bedrooms provided more than enough storage space without disturbing the dust of decades that filmed everything in the attic. He had got quite annoyed with her for bringing the matter up, and it was one of those occasions when Emma had kept her own counsel.

But since then she had had private thoughts about it, and this morning she had needed something energetic to do, something to take her mind off her decision to refuse

Jordan's invitation. Cleaning out the attic had seemed an ideal occupation, and as David was busy with his drawings, she had come up here straight after breakfast.

David was right about one thing, she thought, tracing her name in the dust that thickly covered an old cedarwood ottoman. This was the dust of decades. She doubted Mrs Ingram had ever done more than check for dampness, and she began to wonder whether she might not be more sensible to let well alone. Who knew what hairy monsters might lurk among these piles of outdated magazines and discarded books, the rolls of old wallpaper and battered suitcases, filled with faded curtains and worn-out bedding? She was not normally afraid of insects, but the prospect of meeting spiders or beetles up here sent a shiver down her spine.

Then she gave herself a mental shake. She was being fanciful, she decided impatiently. The attic was just another room, after all, and cleaned out it would make a pleasant storage place for David's old drawings. At present they littered the drawers of his study, but if she could persuade him to let her store them up here, he would have so much more room to work. Besides, it wasn't healthy to have all this dust about the place, and it would give her a great deal of satisfaction to show Mrs Ingram what she had done.

Fortunately she had secured her hair beneath a scarf before tackling the first removals, for the dust flew freely, and she sneezed as particles invaded her nose and tickled her throat. It would be easier, she decided, to investigate the contents of suitcases and boxes up here, rather than drag them through the house, and then those that were to be discarded could all be disposed of together.

Box after box contained toys, she found, and she realised Mrs Ingram must have kept every toy David had ever had. It was a disconcerting discovery, and although she was tempted to throw the lot out, she decided to speak to her mother-in-law first. After all, they were not hers to dispose of, and if Mrs Ingram wanted to keep them, that was her prerogative.

Other boxes contained paint and wallpapering equipment, but after levering off a lid from one of the paint tins and finding only solid glue inside, Emma put the whole lot aside to be thrown away. There was a suitcase full of old photographs that would need to be sorted, and a couple of albums filled with pictures of David growing from a boy into a man. Emma spent a few minutes flipping through these pages, and was shaken when she found Jordan's face staring up at her from a group photograph. It appeared to have been taken when he was at university, but the picture was stuck firmly into the album and she couldn't turn it over to discover whether it was dated. It was unexpected, finding a photograph of Jordan here, and she quickly turned the page to hide his sardonic features from sight. David had been part of the group, too, although he was a couple of years younger than Jordan, and she frowned. She had not known they had attended the same university, or indeed that they had known one another so long.

The shock of even visually encountering the man who had so lately thrown her feelings into turmoil left her taut and vulnerable. The task she had set herself was no longer remote from the problems he had created, and with depression digging at her dwindling enthusiasm, she decided to call it a day. Not even Mrs Ingram's reluctant approval could spur her on at that moment, and the idea of a cup of coffee was far more attractive.

She was picking her way towards the trapdoor when she stumbled over what she saw to be the sleeve of a sweater hanging carelessly over the side of a cardboard box. It was old and dusty and she bent to pull it out and throw it with the other things for disposal. But her fingers encountered something hard within its folds, and as she curiously pulled the fabric aside, an oblong object fell to the floor with a distinct thud.

Frowning, she bent to pick it up and saw with surprise that it was a lady's handbag. Mrs Ingram's? She pulled a face. She didn't think so. It wasn't at all the sort of thing her mother-in-law would use. It was too cheap, for one thing: not leather; and once it had been a garish shade of red.

Whose, then? she wondered, perplexed. It was too modern to have belonged to some long-dead occupant of the house, and besides, the sweater wrapped around it was familiar to her. David had once had a sweater of that colour, with that particular pattern around the welt and sleeves. She hadn't seen him wearing it for ages and ages, but she was sure it was the same one.

Feeling a little like Alice, or maybe Pandora, she turned the clasp fastening and opened the flap. To her surprise the bag was not empty, but filled with the usual paraphernalia to be found in any woman's handbag—purse, make-up, perfume; even some letters and a cheque book. Exactly as if whoever had been using the handbag had lost it. She pulled out one of the letters to read the address and then stared in amazement. The handwriting on the letter was David's, she would have recognised it anywhere, and the addressee was someone called Miss Sandra Hopkins, 11, Montford Street, Stratford. The date on the letter was almost exactly four years ago.

Aware that she was trembling, Emma saw, as if in silent replay, the crumpled wreckage of David's car after the accident that had crippled him. It had been this time of year, the roads frozen and treacherous with black ice. David had been driving to Stratford—to see a client, or so he had said. Emma had never discovered who that client was, but then she had had no reason to disbelieve him. Was it possible he had been going to meet this girl—this Sandra Hopkins? And if so, why hadn't he told her? If he had cared about this girl, why had he insisted on marrying her? And what was more to the point, why was the girl's handbag in their attic, wrapped up in his sweater inside a cardboard box?

'Emma!'

David's angry voice echoed hollowly from the floor below. Since his illness, he seldom ascended to the first floor, even though with two metal sticks he was capable of climbing the stairs. But obviously today he had made that effort, and was presently standing at the foot of the attic stairs, calling up to her.

She was tempted not to answer him. She needed time to absorb what she had just learned in private, but from the tone of David's voice she guessed he was afraid she might have discovered the handbag, and that gave it all a horrible credence.

'Emma! Answer me! I know you're up there. Come on down. I told you not to bother cleaning that place out. It's not necessary.'

Taking a deep breath, Emma tucked the handbag into the waistband of her pants, and lowered herself on to the top step. Then she fitted the trapdoor in place and descended to the landing below where David awaited her. His eyes went instantly to the wedge of red plastic that pushed her chunky sweater aside, and then unbecoming colour stained his pale cheeks.

If Emma had needed any further proof that David knew of the handbag's existence, his guilty appearance was

enough, and pulling it out, she said, rather unevenly:
'I think we need to have a little talk, don't you?'

'It was all your fault!'

The accusation was so unexpected that Emma was speechless. They were facing one another in David's study after he had insisted it was too cold to discuss the matter on the upstairs landing, but now she wondered whether his excuse to go downstairs had been motivated by the desire to gain breathing space. Certainly it was the last thing she had expected him to say, and for a few moments she was so shocked she could only stare at him.

But at last she gathered herself sufficiently to say weakly: '*My* fault?'

'Yes, your fault,' declared David, returning confidence adding assurance to his voice. 'So cold—so frigid! A warm-blooded man could freeze before you'd thaw for him. Such a puritan little soul, I sometimes wondered what——' He broke off abruptly at this point and when he spoke again, she had the distinct impression he was not finishing the sentence in the way he had originally intended. 'I wondered —what kind of a wife you'd turn out to be!'

'Wait a minute.' Emma moistened her lips. 'Are you telling me the—the relationship you obviously had with this girl was the result of my refusal to sleep with you before—before our marriage?'

'What else?' muttered David moodily, and she moved her shoulders in a helpless gesture.

'You can't expect me to believe you!' she exclaimed, a sense of hysteria lifting her voice. 'My God, David, you can't honestly expect me to swallow that!'

'Why not? It's the truth. You were a frigid creature. Still are, most likely. Only I'll never know now, will I?'

The reminder of his physical condition stayed Emma's

reckless impulse to tell him exactly what she thought of his behaviour. Instead, she folded her arms closely about her, and moved almost like a sleepwalker towards the window which looked out on to the walled garden at the back of the house.

'How long was this going on?' she asked, in a tense voice, and David made a sound of irritation.

'Does it matter? It's all over now. It was all over before our marriage——'

'Yes.' Emma swung round. 'I expect it was. But why, I wonder? Because you'd told her that once we were married you intended to be faithful to me?' Her lips twisted. 'Or because the crash curtailed your activities in that direction!'

David's face burned with colour. 'That's a foul thing to say!'

'But more accurate than you care to admit!' declared Emma, without compassion. 'Heavens, to think that all those nights I thought you were working, you were with this—girl, whoever she is! Did anyone know? Did your mother know? Have you both been laughing behind your hands all these years——'

'*No!*' David was adamant. 'No one knew.'

'Sandra Hopkins knew.'

'Yes, well—she got married soon afterwards herself, and as far as I know, she may have moved away from Stratford.'

Emma digested this. Then suddenly she realised she had overlooked the most important thing of all. Why did David have the girl's handbag? What was it doing in the attic, wrapped in his sweater? A film of perspiration broke out all over her. Dear God, he hadn't murdered the girl, had he?

David was watching her, and suddenly she couldn't ask the obvious question. It wasn't that she was scared exactly. She knew David's capabilities, and put to the test, she was probably stronger than he was. He had spent four years practically confined to a wheelchair, and it was unlikely he could harm her in any way. But if there was some reason for his confidence in believing that Sandra Hopkins would not talk about their relationship, she would rather not hear about it from him. She could no longer trust him to answer her honestly, and the sympathy which had kept her affection for him alive had received a mortal blow.

'I know what you're thinking,' he said suddenly, his hands on the wheels of his chair bringing him closer to her. 'You're wondering how Sandra's handbag comes to be in our attic, aren't you?'

Emma moved her shoulders. 'And if I am?'

'The explanation should be obvious.'

'Should it?' Emma was experiencing an increasing sense of unreality. 'I'm sorry, I don't know what you mean.'

'Oh, come on ...' David stared at her. 'Can't you guess? Think of the night of the accident. I'm sure it will occur to you.'

Emma's lips parted. 'She—she was with you!'

'Full marks. Yes, Sandra was with me.' His lips curled. 'For the last time, as you've so prudently pointed out.'

'She—wasn't hurt?'

'Bruised, perhaps. No more.' David's mouth thinned. 'Rough justice, wouldn't you say.'

'But—she left you!'

'Yes, she left me.' David nodded. 'At my request, of course. Unfortunately, she left her handbag behind.'

Emma felt sick. 'But you were badly injured!'

'Oh, spare me the sentimentality!' David swung his chair about. 'You wouldn't understand. You'd never understand, never in a million years! People are *human*, Emma. They have *human* failings.' He glanced at her over his

shoulder. 'Sandra was a real woman, not just a poor imita-
tion!'

Emma flinched. 'Then why did you marry me?'

David uttered a short laugh. 'Why do you think?' He
shook his head. 'I'm not denying that I wanted you, Emma.
I always did. Ever since—ever since ... Well, never mind.
Accept that I did want you, and just because I learned I was
never going to walk again was no reason to call it off. On
the contrary, I needed you then, more than ever.'

Emma felt cold. 'But Sandra——'

'—was a stop-gap, nothing more. Do you think I'd have
married her? Hell, no! I wouldn't marry a woman like
Sandra Hopkins.'

'But you said—she'd got married ...'

'I expect she did. I only said *I* wouldn't marry her.'

Emma expelled her breath on a long sigh. 'That still
doesn't explain how the—the bag got into the attic.'

'Oh, that.' David was offhand. 'As soon as I realised
Sandra had left her handbag behind, I stuffed it into my
briefcase. Then later, after I got home from hospital, I
wrapped it in an old sweater, put it in a box, and got the
window cleaner to throw it up into the attic. I intended to
deal with it later, but I guess I forgot. Besides, no one
ever went up there. Until now.'

Emma shook her head. 'I—I can hardly believe it ...'

David swung round again. 'Then don't. Forget it—I
have. It's all in the past now. It has no bearing on the
present.'

'You can't be serious!' Emma was aghast.

'What do you mean?' David looked suspicious. 'You
can't seriously expect me to believe that this means anything to you now. Good lord, Emma, don't pretend our
association depends on an emotional stability. We both
know we'll never achieve that kind of relationship.'

'No,' she agreed tautly. 'But we could have respect for one another, affection. Unfortunately, right now, I don't seem to feel anything.'

David scowled. 'This is just the excuse you needed, is that it? Has that bloody Avery woman been feeding you with the fruits of independence again? Mother said she was a bad influence, but I defended you. Don't tell me she was right all along.'

'Oh, David, David ...' Emma turned back to stare out of the window. 'Stop blaming other people for your own inadequacy. You can't expect me to learn that you were having an affair with another woman right up to the week of our wedding without feeling something! Some sense of outrage. Can't you understand that?'

'Perhaps you should ask yourself why you couldn't satisfy me yourself!' he countered harshly. 'Let me tell you, I would have done you a favour. Virgins! No man enjoys going to bed with a virgin!'

Emma was glad she wasn't facing him at that moment. A virgin! A hollow description of a hollow defeat. Perhaps he was right—perhaps she was to blame. Perhaps if she had been able to put the memories of Jordan out of her mind, she would have saved him from himself. But if she was honest with herself she would admit that up until the actual hour of her wedding, she had prayed for Jordan to come back to her ...

Now she brushed past him, making for the door. 'I've got vegetables to prepare,' she said, almost inaudibly, but David came after her.

'What are you going to do?' he demanded, and she knew he wasn't referring to the food.

'I don't know,' she replied, not pretending she didn't understand him. 'I have to think.'

'It doesn't make any difference to us, does it?' he ap-

pealed, and she felt the first reluctant pangs of pity returning. But she didn't honestly know, and she had to tell him.

'I have to think,' she insisted, and left him.

Lunch was a silent meal. Despite his professed anxiety,
David ate well, whereas Emma only pushed the fish around
her plate. An awful feeling of being trapped was gnawing
at her nerves, and she knew that whatever happened, she
had to get out of the house this afternoon, away from him.
She couldn't think in his oppressive presence, and the need
for some bread was a heaven-sent reason to walk into town.
Occasionally, in recent weeks, she had offered to push
David's chair into the High Street, but today she omitted
the suggestion and emerged from the house like a prisoner
from the cells.

Inevitably, once she was alone, her thoughts turned back
to Jordan's invitation. Here was the opportunity to ring
him and tell him she could not go with him without either
David or Gilda listening in, but strangely, when she entered
the telephone box, her hand hesitated over dialling his
number. It was as if she shrank from the step that would
make the final break between them, and today, after David's
revelations, she was too raw and vulnerable to suffer his
censure.

She wished she could call on her mother, but after
Emma's marriage Mrs Trace had moved away to live with
her sister in Cumberland, and apart from Christmas and
birthday cards, she made no effort to contact her daughter.

Now, Emma lifted the receiver, listened to the dialling
tone, and then, steeling her fingers, dialled the office
number. The receptionist who answered said she would find
out if Mr Kyle was in the building and asked who was calling. Emma gave her name, and for once was glad it was
Ingram. Trace might have meant something to the girl,
young as she obviously was, but Ingram meant nothing.

It took ten minutes and two further twopences before Jordan's voice came on the line, and then she had to fumble for a further twopence before she could talk to him.

'Where are you phoning from?' he demanded, and when she explained she was in the telephone box outside Abingford's general post office, he added wryly: 'I guess if you're not phoning from home, the answer must be no.'

'Well ...' She still avoided saying the word that would cut him off from her for ever. 'I—I haven't told David.'

There was a pregnant pause, then he said quietly: 'So why are you ringing me? Or have you made up your mind without telling him?'

'I—I—oh, *God*!'

This as the pips started again, and she realised that if she didn't put in another coin they would be disconnected.

'Wait!' Jordan interrupted her frantic search for a two-penny piece. 'Stay where you are and I'll come and meet you. We can't talk like this.' And he hung up before she could protest.

Hanging about outside the phone booth, she felt terribly conspicuous. After all, she had lived in Abingford almost all her life. She knew a lot of people, and a lot of people knew her. What if someone saw her and chose to tell David? Then she pushed such anxieties aside. After the way he had behaved, David could hardly protest about her making a perfectly innocent assignation with a man she had known all her twenty-six years.

She was looking about her for a leather-clad figure when a sleek grey Lamborghini slid to a halt beside the kerb, and Jordan leant across to thrust open the passenger-side door.

'Get in,' he invited brusquely, and rather than attract any further attention, she complied.

The car gathered speed quickly, and beyond the traffic

lights at the end of the High Street it swiftly left the town's
inner boundaries. She thought at first he was taking her to
the factory that was part of the small industrial estate that
occupied part of the outer belt of Abingford, and her nerves
tingled at the prospect of meeting people she knew, and
who had known her father. But instead he turned on to
Mallory Road and just as she turned her eyes away from
the house where she had spent her childhood, he drove
through the gates of Athelmere, the Kyles' rambling old
mansion next door.

Emma's startled eyes met Jordan's enigmatic ones as he
negotiated the narrow drive, overhung now with unpruned
evergreens and the bare branches of the almond trees that
always looked so beautiful in the springtime, and in a
brusque tone he said:

'I thought we could talk here.'

Emma made no response, her attention caught by the
building. The house had originally been built in the eight-
eenth century, but a fire in her great-grandfather's time had
gutted much of the upper floors. The subsequent repairs,
carried out later, had smudged the fine Georgian lines, and
several extensions had added to its air of mixed ancestry.
Neverthless, Emma had always liked it, preferring it to the
neo-Gothic monstrosity next door of which her father had
been so proud. But perhaps that was because of its occu-
pants, she admitted silently. The Kyles had moved in
when she was just a baby, and she had always treated the
house as a second home. There was ivy coating the walls,
framing the square-paned windows, and adding a warming
covering to bare stonework, and her eyes sought the room
above the windows of the dining room which had once been
Jordan's.

Now, the Lamborghini slowed to a halt before the panel-
led door with its familiar fan-shaped window above, and

Jordan swung his legs out of the car. Forestalling any attempt he might have made to assist her, Emma climbed out too, brushing down the skirt of her coat as she turned towards him. Today he had shed the leather coat for a three-piece suit of fine brown suede, and his cream shirt and russet tie were immaculate. The complete business executive, she thought, unable to look at him without fear of betraying her bitterness, and with a faint shrug he mounted the short flight of steps to the door ahead of her.

'Come along,' he advised. 'It's warmer inside. I'll get Mrs Goven to make you some tea.'

'But what will your staff think?' protested Emma, looking up at him then, above her on the steps, and a wry expression crossed his face.

'What staff?' His brows arched. 'You mean the Govens? They are all the staff I retain. I spend so much time— elsewhere, it's not necessary to employ anyone else. Besides, I prefer not to be waited on hand and foot. My socialist background, I suppose.'

There was irony in his tone and Emma knew what he was meaning. It had always been a bone of contention between her father and his that Andrew Kyle had had only a working-class upbringing, and yet was able to meet Jeremy Trace on equal terms. Indeed, it was soon apparent that Andrew had far the better business brain, whereas her father had been hampered by the indolence of his adolescence. Theirs had been a curious partnership in many ways, but despite their differences they had always remained good friends.

Inside the hall of Athelmere, the efficient central heating system dispelled the chilly afternoon air. But looking about her, Emma could not dispel her own feelings so easily, and there was a lump in her throat as she remembered the last time she had stood here. It was the evening her father had put an end to his life, the most terrible evening she was ever likely to experience.

Nevertheless, she endeavoured not to dwell upon the past and she couldn't help but notice the air of shabby melancholy that lay over everything like a film of decay. It was as if no one lived here any more, and observing her expression, Jordan said:

'Like I said, I don't spend a lot of time here. It has— too many memories.'

'Does it?' Emma was surprised. It was not the sort of thing she would have expected Jordan to say, but as if regretting his momentary lapse, he led the way into the library, calling curtly for Mrs Goven.

Across the wood-blocked floor that was badly in need of polishing, the library beckoned like a familiar oasis in a strange desert. In spite of the heating system, someone had lit a fire, and the shadows of the flames danced over leather-bound volumes and worn velvet armchairs. There was Andrew Kyle's desk, still littered with papers as it had been in the old days, and wasn't that his corduroy smoking jacket thrown over the window seat in the rounded bay?

Jordan lit the lamp that stood in one corner, and Emma was hovering just inside the doorway when Mrs Goven came bustling up behind her.

'Oh, Jordan!' she exclaimed, obviously disconcerted. 'I didn't expect you back just yet.'

'I know you didn't, Mrs Goven,' responded her employer, with a wry smile. 'But Mi—Mrs Ingram and I wanted to have a talk and I thought this was the most suitable place.'

'Yes, I see.' Mrs Goven glanced at Emma, and then did a swift double-take. 'Miss Trace!' she exclaimed in astonishment. 'I mean—*Mrs* Ingram, of course.' She shook her head. 'I'm sorry, I didn't realise it was you. How are you? And—and your husband?'

Emma smiled, her fingers tightening round the strap of her handbag. 'I—er—I'm fine, thank you, Mrs Goven. And you? And Mr Goven?'

'Oh, Charlie's all right, miss—I mean, *Mrs*.' She made an embarrassed gesture. 'It's been a long time.'

'Yes, hasn't it?' agreed Jordan dryly. 'Do you think we could have some tea? Mrs Ingram looks frozen.'

'Of course, of course.' Mrs Goven nodded her grey head and hastened out again, bird-like in both looks and movements, and Jordan moved round the desk to close the door and then, to her dismay, stopped right beside Emma.

'Won't you take off your coat?' he asked, making as if to remove it from her shoulders, and she quickly unfastened the leather buttons and shrugged herself out of it.

Jordan took the coat and draped it over the desk, and then indicated an armchair beside the fire. Emma moved towards it jerkily, overwhelmingly aware of his disturbing presence, berating herself for allowing what had happened that morning to shake her normal self-control.

'So ...' Jordan came to stand before her, not sitting down as she had done, but resting one booted foot on the fireside fender, drawing her attention to the taut muscles of his thighs. 'You daren't talk it over with your husband.'

'I didn't say that.' Emma was defensive, and Jordan's mouth turned down at the corners.

'No,' he agreed. 'But all that nervous prevarication over the phone was not intended as an acceptance, was it?'

Emma bent her head. 'I don't know.'

She heard his harsh imprecation. 'What do you mean?' he demanded. 'What don't you know?'

She shrugged. 'I don't know what—what to do.'

'Emma!' He sounded exasperated. 'Either you're coming or you're not. That's all there is to it.'

Emma didn't answer him. It had been that simple once, before the things she had learned about David. Now getting away seemed almost like a lifeline in a wind-torn sea, although she was honest enough to realise that it was not a solution in itself. It had its dangers, too. Jordan might have killed any love she had had for him, but physically he still attracted her, and the line between love and infatuation could become blurred if one moved too close. Yet she was only human, no matter what David might think, and the memories of the relationship she had once had with Jordan still had the power to excite her senses. Was it so unnatural, she asked herself bitterly, when he had been the only man she had ever shared that kind of relationship with?

The return of Mrs Goven with a tray set with teapot, cream jug, sugar basin and cups was a brief diversion, and after Jordan's housekeeper had left them, he suggested that she might help herself.

'Not for me, thank you,' he declined, when she asked his preference, and while she sipped her tea, he poured himself a glass of Scotch from the tray set on his father's desk.

After studying her bent head for a few seconds, he came to take the armchair opposite her, sitting casually on the edge of the seat, legs apart, his hands holding his glass suspended between. It put him more firmly into her gaze and instead of her eyes encountering the crease in the leg of his pants, they rested on the restless brown fingers toying carelessly with the fine crystal.

'Emma,' he said at last, 'you know this is a wasted conversation. You're not going to throw up your job with Gilda Avery or leave that husband of yours for the better part of a week just to go and see my father.'

'You don't know that!' Emma lifted her head indignantly, and then lowered her lids again as those penetrating dark eyes bored intently into hers. 'I—I always cared for—for Uncle Andrew——'

'Don't call him that!' Jordan's voice was abrupt and she was hurt by the harshness of his tone.'You're too old for that kind of foolishness, and making up any relationship that doesn't exist isn't going to make the situation any different.'

'I disagree!' She forced herself to look at him again, trying to ignore the coldness of his eyes, the disturbing familiarity of the planes of his face. 'Your father was like a second father to me. That is, until—until——'

'Until I walked out on you!' said Jordan callously. 'Why don't you say it? It's true. Or do you secretly harbour some belief that it was all a terrible misunderstanding?'

His words were cruel, but instead of breaking her, they gave her the strength she needed. 'How could I imagine that?' she returned sharply. 'I knew *I* wasn't beautiful enough to hold the elusive Jordan Kyle, without the added bonus of Daddy's shares in Tryle Transmissions!'

She saw the way the muscles of his face tightened at her words, bracketing his mouth with deeply drawn lines, and thinning his lips. She waited for the counter-attack, steeling herself against the fury she was sure was to come, and was almost disappointed when it was denied her. Instead, he inclined his head, as if in silent admiration of her outburst, and rising to his feet swallowed the remainder of the Scotch in his glass.

She watched him covertly as he crossed the room to refill his glass, feeling ridiculously contemptible for having said what she had. But it had been the only weapon in her possession, and desperate needs warranted desperate measures. All the same, she had the feeling that in hurting him she was hurting herself more, and the implications of that acknowledgement were more than a little disturbing.

Having replenished his glass to his satisfaction, Jordan returned to his former position on the hearth. Studying the amber liquid through narrowed eyes, he startled her still further when he unexpectedly asked: 'Are you happy, Emma? Has Ingram been a good husband?'

For several seconds Emma was too shocked to answer him, and it was only when she realised he was waiting for her reply that she sought for words to satisfy his interest.

'He—well, I—David has had a hard time adapting to the limitations of life in a wheelchair,' she ventured at last, and felt a quiver of apprehension at the deepening perception of his regard.

'I didn't ask how Ingram was coping with his life,' he retorted quietly. 'I asked whether he's made you happy.'

Emma thrust her teacup aside and rose abruptly to her feet, not realising how close she was to him until her skirt brushed the fabric of his trousers. 'I—I don't see—what my happiness has to do with anything,' she protested. 'As—as a matter of fact, David and I have had quite a good life together.'

'Had?' he probed, raising the glass to his lips without taking his eyes from her. Lowering it again, he wiped his mouth with the back of his hand. 'You talk as if it was over.'

'Do I?' Emma shifted sideways, edging towards the door. 'I expect that's because you disconcert me. As you say, this has been a wasted conversation. And I ought to be going. David will be wondering where I've got to——'

'To hell with David!' Jordan tossed the now-empty glass on to the chair behind him. 'It's you I'm concerned with. I want to know what's making you hesitate about coming with me. If everything was rosy there would be no hesitation, would there?'

Emma held up her head. 'You tell me. You seem to know all the answers.'

'No, I don't.' He thrust his hands deep into his trousers' pockets, tautening the material across his powerful thighs, staring down moodily at the carpet at his feet. 'If anything, I'm confused.' He looked up at her. 'Are you going to enlighten me?'

'What about?' Emma was uncomfortable now, feeling she was getting into deeper water by the minute. 'Jordan, I have to go ...'

'Wait ...' The thick lashes, the only uncharacteristic feature of his hard masculine face, veiled his eyes. 'Tell me, Emma, are you really happy?'

She took a backward step. 'Why do you want to know? What's it to you?'

He hesitated, then he said flatly: 'Call it a—a brotherly interest.'

A brotherly interest!

Emma trembled. He didn't honestly expect her to be able to treat him as a brother, did he? Just being near him like this recalled too well the occasions he had seemed unable to keep his hands off her, when even standing beside her at a party his fingers had been permanently round her wrist, his thumb probing the sensitive skin of her palm. How could she dismiss thoughts like these when she could remember his warmth and his ardour, the feel of his skin against hers, the urgent hardening of his body, and the passion which had swept her far beyond the limits of physical restraint? How could she forget the things he had taught her about herself, even if the lessons she had learned had not all been easy? Looking at him in his immaculate suede suit, the fastidiously buttoned waistcoat concealing the muscular expanse of his chest, she knew a crazy wish that she dared tear the trappings of refinement from him and reduce him to the trembling supplicant he had once been in her arms.

As if aware of her thoughts, his tone roughened as he exclaimed: 'Emma, please! I want to know. Is it such a difficult question to answer?'

Unable to lie to him, she spread her hands in a mute gesture, shaking her head helplessly. 'We—manage,' she conceded tautly. 'Why? Does it give you some sort of perverted satisfaction knowing that no other man has—has——'

She broke off, unable to go on, and dark colour swept up his face. '*No!*' he muttered harshly. 'No. It doesn't satisfy me at all. But for God's sake, why did you marry him? After the way he'd behaved, there was no compunction on your part to compensate the selfish swine!'

Emma blinked at him, staring blankly. Then she gathered herself and whispered in a hoarse voice: 'What—what do you mean? A-after the way he'd behaved? What do you know about David's behaviour?'

Jordan met her agonised gaze, and then with an ungodly imprecation he raked long fingers through his hair, resting his hand impatiently at the back of his neck. 'You *know!*' he insisted. 'You must.'

'What must I know?'

'Oh, for God's sake, Emma!' Jordan paced restlessly across the room, standing staring out the window at the fading light. With his back to her, he was no less disturbing, and her gaze lingered on the width of shoulders that tapered towards his hips. 'Don't pretend you didn't know what kind of a man Ingram was!'

Emma didn't immediately answer him, and he turned slowly to face her, his eyes demanding a response. 'If—if you mean what I think you mean, I—I didn't know——' she was beginning, when the ugly word he used overrode her nervous explanation.

'You didn't know!' he declared. 'But you must have done. Half of Abingford could have told you.'

'Could have told me what?' Emma was feeling distinctly sick now. 'That—that David was having an affair with a girl called Sandra Hopkins?'

'You said you didn't know!' he accused her angrily. 'Are you trying to make a fool of me?'

'No, no.' She shook her head. 'He—I—if you'd let me finish, I would have told you I didn't know until—until this morning.'

'This morning?'

'Yes. I found—I found her handbag in the attic. She—she was with David the night—the night he had his accident, you see, and there were—letters inside. I didn't read them, but they were addressed in David's handwriting.'

Jordan's features were drawn into a scowl. 'I see. And that's all you know.'

Emma gulped. 'What else is there?'

But Jordan shook his head. 'No,' he muttered, almost speaking to himself. 'Why should I tell you? It's nothing to do with me.'

'Jordan!' She went towards him then, her eyes dark and troubled. 'You know you can't leave it there. What else should I know?' She touched his sleeve. 'Please—I have the right . . .'

Jordan bent his head. 'I don't. Ask him yourself. Ask him how the accident happened. You do have *that* right.'

Emma's lashes flickered. 'What do you mean? David was always such a careful driver, particularly on ice. What are you saying? That he was carrying on with—with the girl while he was driving.' She moistened her upper lip. 'She wasn't—injured, was she?'

'Not to my knowledge.'

'Is—is she still living in Stratford?'

'I expect so.' Jordan flexed his shoulder muscles and glanced out the window. 'I'd better take you back, hadn't I? Before it gets dark.'

'Jordan!'

'Don't ask me, Emma. I can't answer you.' He reached past her for her coat and held it towards her. 'Here. It's getting late, and I have a meeting at five o'clock.'

Emma's silent appeal went unanswered, and with a feeling of angry indignation, she pulled on her coat. Then picking up her handbag, she returned to the reason for her being there: 'You haven't asked me whether I'm coming with you. Don't you want to know?'

His sigh was a weary admonition. 'Well?'

'I'm coming,' she announced tautly. 'I'm sorry if you were hoping I'd refuse, but I've decided to accept. Why shouldn't I have some freedom, too? Let everyone pity David, as they've been pitying me all these years!'

CHAPTER FOUR

JORDAN drove her all the way home. In spite of a moment
of weakness in the town when she suggested he might
drop her in the High Street, she retained her mood of reck-
lessness, and when the Lamborghini stopped outside the
house in Mellor Terrace she half hoped David was looking
out of the window.

'Well?' he said, as she made to get out. 'Changed your
mind?'

'No.' She shook her head firmly, although her mouth was
dry. 'Thank you for the lift.'

'It was my pleasure,' he assured her, his eyes lingering
on her hair, and she pushed it back with a nervous hand.
'Can my secretary get in touch with you tomorrow to fix
the details? You'll need a valid smallpox vaccination certi-
ficate, too. You'd better arrange to have that done immediately.'

'All right,' she nodded. 'Anything else?'

He gave her a rather searching look, and then, as if regretting his gentleness, he leant past her and thrust open
her door with suppressed violence. 'There'll be three of us
on the flight,' he said. 'You, me and Stacey. You know
Stacey, don't you? Or rather you'll have seen her, I expect.
She and I are—good friends.'

Emma felt as if he had just delivered a blow to her solar
plexus, and it was all she could do to crawl out of the car
and stand on the kerb as he drove off. Stacey! Stacey Albert, of course. Just as Gilda had predicted.

She felt physically sick, the tea rising like bile in her throat, and to complete her humiliation, the door of the house opened at that moment and David's mother stood there looking down at her, like some avenging angel.

'That was Jordan Kyle's car, wasn't it?' she demanded, as Emma reluctantly climbed the steps towards her. 'What were you doing in *his* car? I didn't know you ever saw him these days.'

'I don't. That is—I didn't. Not until yesterday,' admitted Emma wearily, and brushed past her into the hall.

David was waiting at the drawing room door, and judging by his expression, he too had seen who had brought her home. But unlike his mother, he didn't immediately say anything, and his silence was in some way more ominous than his anger might have been.

'Tea's ready,' announced Mrs Ingram, ushering them both into the drawing room. 'We couldn't wait for you any longer, Emma. Wherever have you been?'

Emma wondered whether it would be easier to break the news to David when they were alone, and then decided against it. David could easily take himself off to his study, as he had done in the past, when he didn't want to listen to what she had to say, and she sensed that right now he was wishing his mother wasn't here. Of course, he had no idea why she had been seeing Jordan, but he had the fore-knowledge of what had happened that morning, and he had had time to build his own defence. He had denied that his mother had known about his affair with Sandra Hopkins, and despite what Jordan had told her, she was inclined to believe him. For one thing, Mrs Ingram would never hear a word said against her son, and if there had been gossip, she would have discounted it.

Now, seated before the fire in the drawing room, Mrs Ingram returned to the subject of Jordan Kyle. 'Emma tells me she saw Jordan yesterday, David. You didn't tell me he had been to visit you.'

'He hasn't,' stated David flatly, accepting the cup of tea his mother had just poured. 'I didn't know Emma saw him yesterday either.'

They both turned to look at her, and Emma quickly set her own cup down on the glass-topped table. 'He—er—he came to the shop,' she volunteered, reaching for a biscuit, although the last thing she wanted to do right now was eat anything. Breaking the biscuit between her fingers, she added, 'His father's very ill. He came to tell me. He knew how—how close Uncle Andrew and I had been in the past.'

Unaware of her son's incensed features, Mrs Ingram snorted. 'If that man's sick, you should be pleased, Emma,' she declared. 'After what he did to your father! If you ask me, justice has been a little late in asserting itself.'

Emma's fists clenched at the woman's callous words, and it was all she could do not to blurt out there and then that Andrew Kyle was more than twice the man her son was. Instead, she schooled her features and said quietly: 'My father had no one to blame but himself. The Kyles had every right to take over the company. My father was a bankrupt, and you know it. The mercy was that he didn't bankrupt the company as well.'

'Andrew Kyle!' sneered Mrs Ingram. 'He was a charlatan. Coming to Abingford from London, buying into your father's business, bringing his East End roughness into a company that was known for its politenes and courtesy.'

'Trace Transmissions was dying, Mrs Ingram, and you know it. Without Andrew Kyle's money, my father would have gone bankrupt years ago.'

'How can you say that, Emma?'

Mrs Ingram was shocked, but David interrupted their exchange by saying shortly: 'You still haven't told us why he brought you home this afternoon. Did you meet him accidentally in town? Or was it a planned arrangement?'

Emma coloured then, but she refused to allow him to subdue her. 'As a matter of fact, I did arrange to meet him,' she replied, much to his obvious amazement. 'But only after I went out. I rang him, you see.'

'You rang him?'

Mrs Ingram gasped, but again David silenced her with an impatient stare. 'Why did you ring him?' he asked. 'Had it anything to do with what happened this morning?' And as her eyes widened now, he added: 'I wouldn't have expected that of you, Emma. What's past is past. Do you think I haven't suffered enough as it is? Knowing how I must have hurt you?'

Looking down at her hands, when she could drag her eyes away from David's triumphant ones, Emma had to admit that he was clever. By bringing the matter up himself, he had successfully spiked any attack she might have made, and already his mother was agitatedly speculating about what might have happened. Of course, David was assuming she had only contacted Jordan in an effort to get even with him, but nevertheless he had drawn her fire and left her on the defensive.

Unable to keep silent any longer, Mrs Ingram exclaimed: 'Emma, what is going on? What happened this morning? Why should you contact Jordan Kyle because of it? Surely you can tell me!'

Before Emma could speak, however, David gave his explanation.

'I'm afraid my wife has found out that before our engagement, I was having an affair with another girl,' he said, astounding Emma by his audacity. 'It was all over, long before we got married, but I'm afraid it is true that at one time I was going out with both of them simultaneously.'

'David!' Mrs Ingram stared at him. 'Who was it? Do I know her?'

'Oh, no.' David shook his head. 'She was just a little typist from Stratford. A pretty little thing, but not really my type at all.'

'David!' It was Emma who spoke now, the words bursting from her. 'How can you tell such lies?' She turned to her mother-in-law. 'Mrs Ingram, what David has told you is true, up to a point. The point is—he was going out with her up until the week of our marriage. She was with him when he had the accident!'

'No!' Mrs Ingram was pale, and she turned back to her son for reassurance. 'Is this true? Is what Emma says true? Because if it is . . .'

'No, of course it's not.' David was brusque, the anger in his eyes directed at Emma. 'It's just a tale made up by my dear wife to justify her reasons for running after Jordan Kyle!'

'How can you say that, David?' Emma was horrified. 'The handbag——'

'What handbag?' Mrs Ingram looked from one to the other of them. 'What handbag is she talking about, David?'

'I really don't know,' drawled David coldly, and too late Emma realised she had left the bag with him when she went out. He must have disposed of it as he had intended to do years ago. And with it her only chance of proving she was not a liar.

'Well?' Mrs Ingram was looking to Emma to explain, but she could only shake her head.

'There was a handbag,' she said. 'A girl's handbag, in the attic. I found it this morning.'

'She's lying!' David's laugh was almost convincing. Certainly it convinced his mother. 'I've told you, this is some ruse to gain your sympathy before she tells us why she was really seeing Kyle.'

'All right.' Emma rose abruptly to her feet, unable to take any more of this without defending herself. 'Believe what you like. And believe this, too. Andrew Kyle is dying, and he wants to see me. *To see me!* But, as you know, he lives in the West Indies. That's why Jordan came to see me. That's why I rang him this afternoon. I'm going with him to Valentia. I'm going to see Uncle Andrew. And nothing either of you can do will stop me!'

A week later, suffering the after-effects of her smallpox vaccination, Emma thought she had never felt lower in spirit. Not even when her father died had she felt this personal sense of bereavement, and only her feelings when she realised Jordan had finished with her compared to the sense of impending disaster she was experiencing now.

It had been a terrible week: a week of rows and re-criminations, a week when David had alternated between efforts to placate her about his own shortcomings and a violent urge to hurt and humiliate her into giving up her resolution to go to the Caribbean. But the lies he had told his mother had been further proof of his desire to protect himself at all costs, and any doubts she had had about her decision had been dispelled by his cruelty and his selfishness.

There had been no need to arrange for anyone to take care of him. As soon as Mrs Ingram learned that her son was to be left on his own for several days, she had immediately volunteered to look after him herself, at once making Emma feel like a visitor in her own home, and an unwelcome visitor at that. Naturally, Mrs Ingram had taken David's side against his wife, although Emma sensed that loyalty played a greater part than conviction. But she cared so fanatically for her son, she paid lip service to his protestations of innocence.

Emma herself gave a little thought to what would happen on her return. Deliberately, she shut such thoughts out of her mind, knowing that divorce might be the only answer. But how could she divorce half a man? she asked herself, and knew she had no answer to give.

Gilda had been kind about giving her the time off. It was not one of their busiest periods, and she insisted she could manage alone. As to Emma's decision to go with Jordan, she had been curiously non-committal about that, and Emma couldn't make up her mind whether this was due to dissention or discretion. The latter had never seemed one of Gilda's strong points, and she had certainly not been enthusiastic when it was first suggested. But maybe she had noticed Emma's pale cheeks and come to her own conclusions about their origins.

Jordan's secretary had telephoned the travel arrangements to her. She sounded young and super-efficient, and Emma guessed he never surrounded himself with inadequate people. The flight they were taking left London at half past one on Friday afternoon and arrived in Barbados soon after six o'clock, their time. The onward flight to Valentia was not to be undertaken until the following morning, and they were to spend the night at an hotel not far from the international airport. Jordan, his secretary said, had business which would keep him in London on Thursday night and therefore it was arranged that Emma should take the early morning train to the capital and make her own way to the airport. Jordan would meet her in the departure lounge of Terminal 3 before one o'clock. Her ticket, so that she could clear passport control, had been delivered to her by messenger, and it now reposed in its folder at the bottom of her handbag.

Emma, absorbed with making the final arrangements for

her journey, had determinedly thought no more about David's accident and its subsequent revelations. She didn't want to know any more about it, she had told herself fiercely, uncaring for the moment that something left un-aired can sometimes decay.

But the night before she was due to leave, David made his final attempt to stop her from going, and she remembered what Jordan had said. Waiting until he paused in his recriminatory accusations, she asked him what Sandra had been doing when the car crashed.

'What do you mean?' To her surprise, David had turned pale, and his bony fingers closed round her wrist in a vice-like grip. 'What have you heard? What's Kyle been saying?'

'Jordan?' Emma frowned. 'What could he say?' Then, when her efforts to free herself did not succeed, she added: 'Except that half the town knew of your affair with the girl. You didn't tell me that!'

David stared at her searchingly, and then let go her hand. 'He's lying,' he declared shortly. 'I was very—discreet!'

'Discreet!' Emma pressed her lips together. 'Oh, David, you don't know the meaning of the word. And as for Jordan lying—you're well qualified to judge, being a liar yourself.'

'For God's sake!' David scowled angrily. 'Let it go, can't you? Hell, if you'd never gone into the attic, you'd never have found the damn bag! Just remember that.'

'But that wouldn't have altered the fact that it was there,' she protested bitterly. 'Can't you see that? If only you'd told me ...'

'Oh, come on ...' David was scornful. 'What would you have done if I'd confessed? Let me cry on your shoulder? No! You'd have walked out on me, just like Kyle walked out on you. And I wasn't having that. I needed you—I still do. And God help me, you'll never get a divorce so long as I'm alive. Don't think you're going to run to Jordan Kyle for sympathy, because you're not!'

Emma sighed. She had revealed that Stacey Albert was going with them in the hope of placating any jealousy on his part, but he sickened her with his crude assertions.

'If,' she said, 'and I admit it's unlikely, I should ever decide I want a divorce, you won't be able to stop me,' she declared, and then gasped in pain and revulsion as his hand thudded against the side of her face.

'Don't you ever say a thing like that to me again!' he snapped savagely. 'You're my wife. Nothing can alter that. And what I have, I keep!'

The departure lounge of Terminal 3 was large and impersonal. Most people occupied their time by queueing for trays of tea or coffee, eating sandwiches they didn't really want to calm their nerves or simply for something to do. Even on this frosty February morning it was a hive of activity, and Emma was glad of the anonymity. With her fur hat pulled down low over her ears, and a scarf hiding the lower part of her face, she was unrecognisable, and she huddled over her own cup of coffee with a feeling of cold isolation.

Occasionally, a pair of male eyes was attracted by the silk curtain of hair that spilled over her shoulders or by the sooty lashes hiding her eyes, but mostly she felt people wondered why she should feel the cold so severely when the temperature in the departure lounge was easily sixty degrees.

Getting to the airport had been no problem. Gilda had insisted on driving her to the station and seeing her on to the train, and apart from her initial horror at the sight of the swelling above Emma's cheekbone, she had said nothing

to disturb her. On the contrary, she had urged her to enjoy herself if it was at all possible, and to get some healthy
colour into that pale face.

David had not even been up when Emma had left the
house, but she had made the effort to say goodbye to him,
an effort which went unrewarded when he turned his face
to the wall and wouldn't speak to her. He didn't even
apologise for the ugly swelling around her eye, and she
closed his door again with an awful sense of finality.

At Euston, she transferred to the underground, taking
the tube right out to Heathrow. It was a simple matter then
of wheeling her luggage along the walkways to the international air terminal, and checking in at one of the British
Airways desks. With her luggage disposed of, she was free
to clear passport control and wait until the flight was
called. Her ticket was first class, the first time in her life
she could remember travelling so expensively, and she wondered whether she ought to offer Jordan the cost of her fare.
To do so would just about clear her bank balance, but perhaps he expected her to. After all, several hundred pounds
meant nothing to him, not when he could pay for her fare,
his own, and no doubt for Stacey Albert's as well.

She glanced at her watch. Twelve-fifty, she acknowledged
tensely. Ten minutes to one. The flight was likely to be
called at any moment. A swift examination of the departure
board supplied the information that theirs was indeed the
next flight on the rota, all flights listed above it having
already reached the 'Now boarding' or 'Last Call' fre-
quencies.

'Emma!'

She looked up reluctantly to find Jordan standing beside the table, his brown leather coat unbuttoned to reveal
the dark blue corded suit beneath. He was carrying a briefcase, and his light hair was dampened with what appeared

to be rain. He was alone, and for a moment her heart raced with painful intensity, but then he drew out a chair and sat down beside her, adding lightly: 'Stacey's gone to the ladies' room. Flying always affects her that way.'

'Oh!' Emma looked down into her coffee, willing him not to stare at her too closely, and with an impatient sigh he exclaimed:

'What's wrong? No last-minute hold-ups, were there? You found your way here without difficulty?'

'Oh, yes. Yes,' Emma nodded, her voice muffled in her scarf. 'I—er—I took the tube.'

'*Fly the Tube*, eh?' he remarked dryly, quoting the current slogan British Rail were using to advertise this new method of getting out to the airport. 'I bet you're the only first class passenger that came that way.'

He was trying to be casual, she knew that, to put her at her ease and remove the stiffness that had developed between them at their last meeting. But she couldn't relax, and she was very much afraid he would put the wrong interpretation on her behaviour. But how could she show him her face and tell him that David had placed his final sign of disapproval upon her? It would be so humiliating. She could only hope he would be so involved with Stacey throughout the journey that by the time he did notice her the swelling might have subsided.

She heard him expel his breath rather harshly, and then, in a low angry voice, he said: 'For heaven's sake, why are you all wrapped up like that? It's not cold in here. What are you trying to do? Avoid being recognised with me?' And before she realised his intention, he had pulled the fur hat from her head and exposed the ugly contusion below and around her left eye.

'Oh, God!' His irreligious ejaculation contained both sympathy and anger in equal measures. 'Emma ...'

Involuntarily, his hand was extended towards her, his fingers moving almost tenderly across the puffed and purple skin. His touch was a caress and they both knew it, and when his fingers moved to her lips, they parted automatically.

'*Ingram!*' he said, between clenched teeth. 'I'll kill him!'

His dark eyes probed hers with increasing intensity, and then, when she was lost to everything but the devastating intimacy of his gaze, a chair was pulled out between them, and a bright, artificial voice asked:

'Is this a private party, or can anyone join in?'

Immediately Jordan rose politely to his feet, but the white line around his mouth took longer to disappear, and it was left to Stacey to introduce herself.

'I say,' she exclaimed, after she had announced her name and professed knowledge of Emma's, 'that is a nasty bruise you've got there! No wonder Jordan was so uptight. He never strikes a woman, do you, darling?'

'What?' Jordan made an obvious effort to assert himself. 'Oh, no. No.' He forced a grin. 'At least, not to date.'

Stacey smiled up at him, taking his hand and clinging to it. 'Sit down again, darling. Don't stand on ceremony. I've completed my ablutions, and if I have to meet my maker, at least my lipstick is on straight.'

'Our flight's been called,' remarked Jordan, indicating the board behind her. 'We can get on the plane, if you like.'

'Oh ...' Stacey glanced over her shoulder. 'Oh, so it has. But darling, first class passengers don't need to join the queue. Couldn't I have a little drink first? Like a double vodka and tonic, for instance?'

'You can get a drink on board,' retorted Jordan firmly. 'Emma: are you ready?'

Emma nodded, jamming the fur hat back on to her head again, and getting to her feet she followed the others across to the departure gates. The long corridor stretched away ahead of her, and she felt a twinge of apprehension. It was years since she had been in an aeroplane, and then only to the continent. She had never crossed the Atlantic before, and her knees trembled. But Jordan was striding confidently ahead with Stacey beside him, trying to keep up with him, and she hastened after them. She was committed now, and there was no turning back.

The flight was uneventful. The aircraft was not full, and Emma had the two seats on her row to herself. Jordan sat behind with Stacey and apart from an occasional giggle from the other girl, she would scarcely have known they were there. A covert glance over her shoulder essayed the knowledge that his briefcase had not been an affectation, and he spent the journey studying the files he had brought with him. Stacey slept, curled up beside him like a kitten, the blonde head resting on his shoulder apparently no annoyance to him.

Emma could not sleep. She had accepted a magazine from the stewardess, but she hardly glanced at it, although the view from the window was of little interest to her. Acres of cloud beneath them gave way to the distant haze of the ocean, but from several miles up it was impossible to see anything. It was boring really, although because of her own fears and apprehensions Emma felt far from that innocuous state.

For the first time she let herself think about the man she was flying all these miles to see, without the constant strain of uncertainty. Until now, there had always been the possibility that something would happen to prevent her trip, but high above the south Atlantic she could contemplate their meeting without any complications. It brought the seriousness of his condition into complete focus, and she couldn't help wondering what had driven him to send for her. Was it only a desire to see her, or had he some notion of reuniting her and Jordan? Surely, as he knew she was married he could not be thinking along those lines. And yet it was strange that he should think of her at a time like this. He had always been in favour of their relationship in the old days, but that was before the break-up of the partnership ...

Throughout the lunch and dinner that were served during the flight, Emma was extremely selfconscious of her bruised appearance. But the steward and stewardesses were paid to be discreet, and apart from their initial reaction they made no reference to it. On the contrary, by the end of the flight Emma had almost forgotten it herself, until she went to the tiny toilet compartment and glimpsed her face in the mirror.

It was still light when they landed at Seawell. For the past hour or so the aircraft had been slowly descending towards a sea as blue as any Emma had ever seen, splashed about with islands that seemed to rise in peaks from the translucent water. Here and there, she glimpsed a beach, with sand that looked white from the air, and the billowing sails of a yacht that moved smoothly across the calm waters. Circling above Barbados, she could see its greenness, and as they dropped lower, the settlements spread out across the island.

The airport formalities were soon dealt with, but the heat was almost an assault. In her knee-length boots and suede coat, Emma felt stifled, and the idea of wearing the fur hat and scarf had to be abandoned.

'We'll take a cab to the hotel,' Jordan explained, walking between the two women as they left the Customs hall. 'I can ring my father from there and make arrangements for the Cessna to come and pick us up tomorrow.'

Stacey fanned herself with her hand. Like Emma, she

had been wearing a warm coat, but presently her fur was draped over Jordan's shoulder, and she had unfastened the neck of her cream silk blouse. With her golden hair blowing in the faint breeze that drifted off the ocean and her perfect features lifted to the sun, she looked like some exotic model girl, Emma thought, overwhelmingly conscious of the shortcomings of straight dark hair and a sallow complexion. The bruised eye didn't help, but she acknowledged that even without it she couldn't hold a candle to the beautiful Miss Albert.

The drive to their hotel was not long, but curving along the coast road as it did, they were given a magnificent view of the sun sinking into the horizon. Night fell quickly on the island, and by the time they had checked into their rooms it was quite dark. As Emma shed her clothes to take a longed-for shower in her bathroom, she could hear the persistent piping of what she later learned was a tree frog, and experienced her first real feeling of excitement, of something unexpected about to happen.

Jordan had suggested that as it was already ten o'clock-plus by the time they were used to, she should have a light meal served in her room instead of dressing and going down for dinner, but Emma couldn't help wondering if that was what he and Stacey would do. There was a tightness in her chest when she contemplated what the culmination of their evening might be, and she determinedly ran the water cold in the shower to rid herself of any thoughts of that kind.

Deciding not to dress, she put on a light cotton wrapper after her shower and was drying her hair with a towel when a black-skinned waiter brought her a crisp chicken salad and some fresh fruit.

'Mr Kyle said this would be suitable, Miss Ingram,' he explained, setting the tray on the table beside her. 'The pot contains tea, not coffee. Is that all right?'

'It's fine, thank you.' Emma nodded, wondering what the waiter was making of her face, and decided not to correct him about her married state. The last thing she wanted was for him to think she was running away with Jordan, perhaps escaping from a brutal husband. 'Er—what time is breakfast?'

'Any time you like between seven and ten,' replied the man with a grin. 'But you'll be awake long before then, I expect. The trip west is always easier to adjust to than the trip east.'

Emma returned his smile and he withdrew after assuring himself that the tray was set to his satisfaction. Emma wasn't hungry, but it was kind of Jordan to do this for her, and she was tempted to ring his room and thank him. But suspecting that Stacey might be with him, she decided not to bother. If he was sleeping with the girl, she'd rather not know about it.

With her hair dry, she turned out the lights and opened the windows on to her balcony. Without the light to attract them, the night insects were much less of an annoyance, and the air was pleasantly cool as it probed inside the open neckline of her wrapper. She wouldn't wear her nightgown tonight, she thought with sudden daring. It was too warm, and besides, it would prove that for the next few days at least she was her own mistress. *Her own mistress!* She folded her arms about her. It was ironic that the last time she and Jordan had been together, if he had not been stronger-minded than herself, she would have been his!

CHAPTER FIVE

SHE was still standing there, gazing out at the dark ocean as it moved in silent infinity along the curving shoreline, when there was a sudden tap at her door. At first she thought she had mistaken it, the sounds of the hotel clearly audible at this hour of the evening when most people were preparing to go down for dinner. She could even hear the sound of an orchestra playing in the distance, and guessed the hotel catered handsomely for its three hundred or so guests.

So she didn't immediately respond to the tapping, and only when it was repeated and Jordan's low voice demanded: 'Emma! Emma, are you there?' did she hasten across the room and switch on the light before opening the door.

'Jordan!' she exclaimed, half alarmed by her own reaction to him, and supporting himself against the doorpost with one hand, he said: 'Can I come in?'

He, too, had showered, judging by the dampness of his hair, but he had dressed again in the navy corded pants he had worn to travel in and a clean silk shirt. He looked tired and slightly drawn, as if he had worked too hard on the journey, but the dark eyes were as alert as ever.

'Of course,' Emma said now, standing back to allow him admittance, but she cast a swift look up and down the corridor outside before closing the door again.

'It's all right,' he said dryly. 'I wasn't observed. What are you afraid of? Your reputation or mine?'

79

'Neither,' she denied quickly, tucking her hands into the wide sleeves of her robe, wishing she was wearing something a little more inspiring and a little less revealing. 'I thought perhaps—Miss Albert might be with you.'

'Call her Stacey,' advised Jordan flatly. 'Everyone does.' Then he crossed the room and closed the french doors before a whole army of moths could launch their attack on her lamp.

'Wh-where is she?' Emma asked, as much for something to say as anything, and remembering her damp hair, she lifted her hand to twist it into a coil on the nape of her neck.

'Don't . . .' he said, almost involuntarily, and then, as her hand dropped, he added: 'I see you got your salad.'

'Oh—yes, thank you,' Emma nodded. 'I'm not hungry right now, but I might have it later.'

'I expect you're tired,' Jordan agreed. 'I am, too. But I—I had to talk to you.'

'Yes——' Emma tried to sound casual, but it was difficult when her heart was thumping in her ears, and every sense in her body was supremely aware of the warm smell of his.

'Yes.' He ran his hand down the opened neck of his shirt. He was not an excessively hairy man, but there was a light covering of fine hair just below his collarbone, and his fingers curled against the sun-brown skin. Covering the space between them, he halted before her, and as once before, his free hand stroked her cheek. 'Emma, why did Ingram do this to you? Was it something I said? I have to know. It's driving me off my head!'

Emma's eyes were mesmerised by the restless curling of his nails against his chest, but she managed to say jerkily: 'No—no, it was nothing you said. It—it was something I said actually. He—he doesn't like me to be—independent.'

'*Independent!*' Jordan stared down at her, his dark eyes

probing hers with increasing intensity. 'Surely it's he who's the dependent one. Emma, are you sure that's all it was?'

'What else could it be?' Emma took a step back from him so that he was forced to drop the hand that was touching her cheek. 'Don't worry about it. It wasn't important. Except—except that your father's going to wonder what's happened.'

Jordan's nostrils flared, but the words of protest she saw in his face were never uttered. Instead he inclined his head as if acknowledging his dismissal. But when he moved towards the door she found she didn't want him to go, and almost recklessly she stepped into his path. His brows drew together into a frown, but before he could say anything she burst out:

'Can I ask you something, Jordan?' And as he narrowed his eyes, she hastened on: 'You've asked me a question. Now let me ask you one: why—why did you walk out on me? Was it because it was no longer necessary to keep up the pretence, or because Daddy committed suicide? Or was there something else? Did I do something—something so terrible that—that——'

'It was none of those things!' he declared harshly, and she stared up at him through bewildered eyes.

'No?'

'No.' He moved his head slowly from side to side.

'Then what——'

'It doesn't matter.'

'It does matter.' She swallowed with difficulty. 'Look, I've realised you didn't love me. You don't have to pretend about that. But did it have to end so abruptly? So coldly?'

'I *did* love you!' he groaned suddenly, grasping her by her shoulders with hands that cut through the frail barrier of her robe. 'I did love you. I still do. I expect I always will, although I know you'll find that hard to believe.' But, as she swayed towards him, he shook her with a violence that sent her hair tumbling wildly about her shoulders and left her neck almost too weak to support it. 'But that love has changed. What I feel for you now is the love I would feel for—for a sister! Now do you understand?'

Her mouth was dry. 'And you don't make love to a sister.'

'No.' His jaw muscles worked tautly. 'It—it was different before. You got under my skin. And God help me. I didn't want—I didn't *try* to resist you!'

Emma couldn't take this in. What was he saying? That when her father died he had realised that what he felt for her was only the love of a sister! She couldn't believe it. It didn't make sense. Why, only the night before her father died, they had talked of marriage ...

He was staring down at her now, and there was anguish as well as a curious kind of anger in his face. Lips parted, she gazed back at him, trying to read his expression, the bewilderment in her face giving it a pure and sensitive vulnerability. Wide-eyed, she was entreating his sympathy and understanding, unaware of the delicate appeal of those parted lips, of the limpid beauty of eyes drowned with emotion, of the provocative sensuality of the swelling peaks of her breasts, clearly outlined against the thin material of her robe.

'Emma!' He spoke her name, although it was a strangled sound, and as if he was unable to keep her at arm's length any longer, he pulled her close to him. 'Emma, I don't want you to look at me like that—as if you hated me! I want us to be—to be friends.'

'*Friends!*' With her face pressed against the opened neck of his shirt, when she spoke the hair on his chest invaded her lips. 'Jordan, I don't hate you. You don't hate someone just because you don't understand them ...'

'What do you do, Emma?' he demanded hoarsely, tipping her face up to his. 'What do you do when all your senses—all your instincts—compel you to do something that you know is wrong?'

'You mean—because I'm married,' she began painfully, but he broke in on her forcefully,

'No!' he exclaimed. 'That doesn't signify. I know you only married Ingram in an effort to get even with me!'

'To—get even with you?' she echoed faintly, and his hands moved restlessly in the small of her back, loosening the cord of her robe so that only the pressure of his body against hers kept it in place.

'All right then,' he amended. 'To make me jealous. To show me you could easily put another man in my place!'

'Is that what you think?' She shook her head helplessly. 'Jordan, why should I think I could make you jealous? You didn't even care that I was alive!'

'That's not true. I always cared. Only——' He broke off abruptly, the lines beside his mouth more deeply etched than before. 'You don't understand,' he muttered grimly. 'But soon ...'

Her hands against his chest curled anxiously. She knew they were no barrier to the nervous energy she could feel inside him, the tension that was coiled like a spring, just waiting to be released. And still he held her, not kissing her or caressing her, just holding her in his arms until they both knew it was too late to draw back.

'How long has it been, Emma?' he was asking now, his voice low and urgent. 'How long—since I held you like this? Do you remember that summer? Those nights on the river? Do you remember the houseboat? Those parties—when all I could think about was getting you alone, letting you do what you're doing to me right now?' His hands on her hips created an intimacy between them she remembered too well, and he added thickly: 'You know what you're doing, don't you? You can feel it. And God help me, I want more—much more than *this*——'

Her protest, and it was a feeble thing at best, went for nothing beneath the demanding pressure of his mouth. His hand at the nape of her neck compelled her forward, and the unspoken words opened her lips to his. The urgent reasons why he should not be holding her like this, pillaging her mouth with the sensuous expertise of his, were briefly forgotten, and she lost all sense of time beneath the probing caress of his hands.

If he had been rough or violent, assaulting her savagely and taking what he wanted without sensitivity, she might have stood some chance against him. As it was, the pressure increased gradually, hardening into the hungry passion she had once been eager to assuage. He moulded her body to the throbbing contours of his, making no attempt to disguise how she had aroused him, and slowly, inevitably, her whole being came alive to the demands he was making upon it.

'I *need* you.' His words were delivered with curious desperation, and opening her eyes Emma could see the expression of torment that was twisting his face. 'I do, I do,' he repeated, but he was drawing back from her as he said it. 'I want you. I want to love you,' but his hands pressing her away from him belied his words. Then he spoke again, and Emma's world crumbled at his bitterness. 'I should have known this would happen. Married or otherwise, I should never have let the old man persuade me to bring you out here!'

Emma's breath came out in a trembling gasp, but she subdued the impulse to scream her frustration at him. 'Thank—thank goodness one of us has some sense, then,' she managed to say chokingly. 'At least you remembered I was married. I—I had almost—forgotten.'

'*Emma!*'

As she would have jerked away from him, he caught the lapels of her robe and the careless gesture sent the cord rippling free. At once the wrapper parted, exposing the lissom length of her body, the full breasts and curving hips, the long shapely legs, and the sight of her robbed Jordan of his last vestiges of control.

'Emma,' he groaned hoarsely, 'oh, Emma, come here——' and compulsively his hands slid beneath the robe to draw her towards him.

The sight of his head bent to caress her breast with his lips filled her with a destructive kind of satisfaction. Destructive, because his reminder of her married state had chilled the blood in her veins and left her cold. Yet it was gratifying to know that Jordan still found her desirable, so desirable he was prepared to abandon the girl he had brought with him for her bed.

'Do you want to stay here, Jordan?' she asked, in a low husky voice. 'Do you want to sleep with me?'

He lifted his head, his eyes drowsy with emotion, and for a moment she was almost tempted to forget everything but his obvious need of her. It would be so easy to tumble into bed with him, to let him have his way with her, and experience the rapturous satisfaction only his possession could bring.

But there was too much between them, too many bitter nights and days when she had prayed for even the sound of his voice on the telephone or the glimpse of his lean face through windows clouded by her tears. And as he had pointed out, she was married, *married*, and what he wanted from her had nothing to do with love.

'Emma,' he breathed, and his eyes were narrowed and

sensual. 'Will you let me stay? Is that what you're saying? Dear God, don't tease me!'

And suddenly she was afraid of what might happen, of what she might not be able to control.

'No,' she said now, and pushing his unresisting hands aside, she wrapped the robe closely about her once more. 'I was curious, that's all. A woman's prerogative.'

There was an ominous silence, when the air between them fairly crackled with antagonism, and then Jordan's features hardened into the polite mask he habitually wore. Almost visibly he withdrew from her, and the slight bow of his head he gave her was inexplicably insolent.

'I think you'd better go,' she declared, avoiding looking at him at all. 'I—I'm tired. I'd like to get some sleep.'

'And will you?' he enquired coldly, moving past her towards the door. 'Will you sleep—or will you remember that it was *I* who chose not to take you when you were hot and willing, *Mrs* Ingram?'

From the air, the island of Valentia was a mount of green rising from an encircling border of white lace. Lower, it was possible to see the terraced hillside, and how one side of the island was flatter than the other. It was here that the Cessna came down on a baked earth runway that gave a far from comfortable landing.

The airport buildings consisted of a utility-type building, and a hangar, which Jordan explained to Stacey was used to house the aircraft. It seemed that the Cessna belonged to Andrew Kyle, and its pilot divided his time between flying the plane and chauffeuring his employer about the island.

Emma observed her surroundings without enthusiasm. She had not slept well at all after Jordan's abrupt departure, and his cruel words had bitten deep into the shell of indifference she was trying to assume. It was useless trying to pretend to herself that she had hurt him and that his words had been a kind of defiance. All she knew was that once again she had allowed him to make a fool of her.

The morning had brought no miraculous cure for her depression. She awakened with the sense of something unpleasant hanging over her head, and not even the thought of seeing the man she had always called 'Uncle' Andrew again could dispel her feelings of despondency.

She had breakfast in her room, and by the time she made her way downstairs, Stacey and Jordan were already awaiting her in the foyer. The other girl looked radiant this morning, and Emma couldn't help thinking that no doubt Jordan had released all his pent-up frustration with her. Imagining him with Stacey was pure torment, and she was sure her bitterness was visible in her face for all to see.

At least the swelling around her eye had almost disappeared, and careful make-up had disguised most of the bruising. She left her hair loose for once and it spilled forward over the sides of her face, a dark curtain to hide the dark thoughts she was plagued by.

Stacey had chosen to wear a scarlet jump suit for the trip to Valentia, a clinging garment that exposed most of her smooth white shoulders. Emma guessed the other girl would not tan easily with that fair skin, but no doubt she knew all the best lotions and ointments to use. Emma herself was wearing a plain cream smock with only a narrow band of embroidery around the elbow-length sleeves and the hem, but the loose style suited her, and her olive skin was not so sensitive to the glare of the sun.

Jordan had scarcely spoken to her this morning. In truth, he hadn't spoken a lot to Stacey either, but she was not a girl one could ignore, and her inconsequent chatter made up for Jordan's taciturnity. He, for his part, helped the porter to carry the cases out to the car which was to take them to the airport, and then absorbed himself in the contents of his briefcase as soon as they were airborne. This morning he had shed his formal suit for denims and a body shirt, the close-fitting clothes accentuating his lean masculinity. His bare forearm with its liberal covering of fine hair rested on the arm of his seat only two feet from Emma's own, and time and again her reluctant gaze was drawn to that brown skin and the muscles that moved beneath.

Standing on the airstrip, waiting while Jordan spoke to the pilot and arranged their transport to his father's house, Emma had her first real glimpse of the ocean at close quarters. Beyond the belt of palms that separated them from the curving arc of a cove, the shifting turquoise waters of the Caribbean spread fingers of creaming surf upon the sand, glistening with translucent brilliance. It was an unbelievable scene after the rain-wet coldness of England, and Emma felt an unwilling feeling of excitement stirring inside her. Then Jordan's voice bidding her to follow them broke into her reverie, and its coldness achieved what he had intended. She was not here to dream about warmth and beauty. She was here because he had been compelled to bring her.

The car which was to take them to Andrew Kyle's house awaited them on the road. It was a vintage convertible, with sleek cream lines, and genuine brass headlamps. Smiling, Jordan took the wheel with an admiring Stacey beside him, while Emma got into the back with the black-skinned chauffeur who had been introduced as William. The pilot, who himself acted as chauffeur when the occasion demanded it, was left behind to look after the Cessna and Jordan drove them the three miles or so to his father's villa.

The road was narrow and overhung with vines and creepers in places where the clumps of trees grew close to the track. It rose quickly to several hundred feet above sea level, and then, rounding a bluff with the whole of the west side of the island spread out below them, it descended again towards a building that sprawled over a narrow plateau above a natural cove. There was a yacht lying at anchor in the cove, and the scene was so much like a film set that Emma had to stifle her involuntary exclamation of delight.

As they drew nearer, Emma could see the marble-smooth lawns that surrounded the house, the tumbling riot of colour in the flower beds, and before the shaded verandah, a stone fountain that spouted water into a round basin. The sound of the car's engine disturbed the peace of the morning, and the birds chattered noisily, startled by the unwelcome intrusion.

A man rose from his seat on the verandah as the convertible came up the curving drive towards the house, and came down the shallow steps to meet them. Even after all this time, Emma would have known Andrew Kyle anywhere, despite the fact that he was much thinner than she remembered him, and his tall frame stooped a little from the shoulders. His hair, so like Jordan's still, was grey now, but his eyes were as alert as ever, glittering in his face that was uncannily like his son's. His cotton trousers hung on his hips as he walked towards the car, and the open neck of his shirt displayed the angular hollows between the bones of his throat. Emma's throat felt unaccountably tight as she looked at him, and although he greeted his son and his girl-friend first, his eyes went straight to her.

'Emma!' he exclaimed at last, when politeness had been satisfied. 'Emma, my child! How good it is to see you.'

Emma allowed him to help her down from the convertible's rear seat, and then was embraced with evident warmth and enthusiasm. His emotionalism was unexpected somehow, but her response to it was not.

'It's good to see you—Andrew,' she said, suddenly unable to call him by the childish appellation which had annoyed Jordan so much, and was aware of *his* eyes upon her, watching their exchange.

'Come along, come along,' Andrew said now, leading the way up to the verandah, and Jordan went past him into the house, calling for one of the servants as he went. Andrew looked after his son with apparent pride and admiration, and then turned back to Emma again and bade her sit down on one of the low cushioned loungers.

Stacey, unused to being ignored, made herself comfortable without invitation, and then gesturing towards the magnificent view of the cove below the shelving line of the cliff, she exclaimed: 'I can understand why you live here, Mr Kyle. Who'd exchange Purgatory for Paradise?'

Andrew cast a reassuring smile in Emma's direction, then he transferred his attention to his other guest. 'Yes, it is beautiful, isn't it? I never tire of sitting here. But then I'm an old man. I don't think you'd be able to stand the quietness for long. There's nothing to do here.'

'Ah, but Bridgetown isn't too far away, is it?' countered Stacey, pleased to have gained his interest. 'I mean—if one had a helicopter, one could be in Barbados in less than an hour.'

'A little more than that,' remarked Jordan dryly, coming through the open doors at that moment. 'I've asked Maggie for some coffee,' he told his father casually, walking to the rail of the verandah and resting both hands upon it as he, too, admired the view. 'And some beer. I could surely use a drink.'

'Was the flight uneventful?' enquired Andrew, taking his seat beside Emma and giving her another warm smile. 'Have you ever flown the Atlantic, my dear?'

'No——' began Emma, when Stacey chimed in again: 'I have, lots of times. But strangely enough, I've never been to the West Indies before.'

As Andrew politely asked what she had thought of the United States, Emma digested her words with reluctant relief. So Stacey hadn't been to Valentia before. She had naturally assumed she had.

The whisper of trolley wheels brought Emma's head round with a start, but it was only a black-skinned woman wheeling out a tray of coffee above a refrigerated cabinet containing the beer. For an awful moment she had thought David was there behind her, and dry-mouthed, she found Jordan's eyes upon her. He had seen her involuntary reaction, but fortunately, the others didn't appear to have done so. For a disturbing moment his cold dark eyes held hers with deliberate mockery, and then he moved forward to speak to the woman.

'Allow me to introduce you to my father's guests, Maggie,' he remarked with what Emma sensed to be intentional irony. 'Stacey, Emma: this is Maggie, my father's housekeeper. Maggie—Miss Albert—*Mrs* Ingram.'

The woman, Emma guessed her age to be around forty-five, offered a tentative smile. In an attractive blue overall and white shoes, her curly dark hair cut close to her head, she looked kind and understanding, and Emma wondered whether she knew of her employer's terminal condition. It seemed likely. Jordan obviously treated her like one of the family, and the smile she bestowed on him was warm and affectionate.

The coffee Maggie had prepared for them was the best Emma had ever tasted. It was strong and aromatic, and combined with cream made the most refreshing of beverages. Emma drank hers eagerly, glad of the stimulation it engendered, trying not to speculate on the reasons why

Andrew Kyle had brought her out here. The others talked together casually, Stacey doing her best to remain the centre of attraction, and presently Andrew suggested that the girls might like to be shown their rooms and have time to rest a while before lunch.

'But I'm not tired!' Stacey protested at once, and Jordan interposed gently that what his father really meant was that he would like to rest before the meal. 'Oh, yes. Of course.' Stacey sounded awkward for once, and Andrew took it upon himself to reassure her.

'I'm an old man,' he declared, without rancour. 'You and Jordan can go down to the beach if you like, maybe even take a swim. I'll see you all at one o'clock.'

Maggie appeared, to show their guests to their rooms, and as Jordan didn't need that service he settled himself in the chair Stacey had vacated, and slid smoked glasses on to his nose. Stacey looked back at him lingeringly as she followed Maggie into the house, and Emma guessed she would waste no time indoors.

Their rooms were next door to one another on the first floor. Both rooms possessed a bathroom and both opened on to a balcony that ran along the full width of the house, divided by creeper-hung trellises. The view was the same as that from the verandah below, and Emma realised the balcony was directly above.

Maggie showed Stacey into her room and then accompanied Emma to hers. Her suitcase had been brought up by the stalwart William and presently reposed on the ottoman at the foot of the four-poster bed, and the open doors of the balcony sent the wild silk curtains moving with the draught. The floor was coolly tiled and strewn with rugs, but the predominant colour in the room was cream—cream walls, cream figured bedspread, cream curtains. A bowl of red and cream roses adorned the dressing table, and their perfume mingled with the scents from outside to give the room a fragrance all its own.

Emma shook her head helplessly, moved by the simple beauty of it all, and Maggie gazed anxiously at her. 'You do not like it?'

'Like it? Oh, yes. Yes!' Emma turned to her, eager to correct her impression. 'I love it, thank you. It's—beautiful.'

Maggie smiled, relieved, and flicked a speck of dust from the table beside the bed. 'I am glad. It was Mr Kyle's wish that you should be most comfortable. Now, is there anything else I can get for you?'

Again Emma shook her head, turning round slowly, almost bemused by her surroundings. 'No, nothing, thank you, Miss—Miss——'

'Maggie will do,' returned the woman easily. 'Lunch is at one, as no doubt Mr Kyle has already told you. You can find your way?'

'I think so.'

Emma returned her smile and Maggie left her to go about her own business. With the door closed, the balcony beckoned, and she moved towards it almost compulsively. She was here. She was actually here on Valentia, she thought incredulously. She was staying in Andrew Kyle's house, and soon now she would have to assure him that she and Jordan were no longer estranged. A ridiculous whim considering their attitudes to one another ...

Thinking of Jordan made her realise that where he was sitting on the verandah was almost exactly below where she was standing at this moment. What was he thinking? she wondered. What had been his reaction when his father first put the idea of bringing her out here to him? And why did he pretend he loved her when it was obvious he despised her? A shiver ran down her spine. Something told her that in his anger he could be far more formidable than David, and last night he had been very angry with her indeed. Physical violence would play no part with him; he had far more destructive weapons in his grasp, but it was up to her not to let him know it.

CHAPTER SIX

EMMA unpacked her suitcase and put its contents away in the drawers of the dressing table and in the tall polished wardrobe that stood against the wall. Then she took off her dress and went into the bathroom to wash.

The bathroom was tiled with squares of cream-veined marble inlaid with tiny red rosebuds. The bath was deep, and of the step-in variety, while an adjoining shower was cubicled in fluted glass. There were mirrors beside the bath and above the washbasin, and a fluffy rug to stand on while one got dry.

Emma contented herself with a wash in cool water, and was drying her face on one of the rich cream towels when a voice hailed her from the bedroom. Imagining Maggie must have forgotten something, Emma went to the bathroom door, and then stared in surprise at Stacey making herself comfortable on the side of her bed. Her appearance could not have been more unexpected, and Emma felt a wave of hot colour sweeping up her cheeks at the awareness of being caught in only bikini-brief cotton panties. Fortunately the towel she still held to her face concealed the upper half of her body, but all the same, she didn't care for the other girl's careless appraisal.

'Hi,' declared Stacey indifferently, unconcerned by Emma's embarrassment. 'You don't mind me joining you, do you? Jordan's asleep and I've got nothing to do.'

Emma continued to hold the towel in front of her, hardly knowing what to say, and Stacey heaved an exaggerated sigh. 'For heaven's sake, stop behaving like an outraged virgin! Put your clothes on, if you want to. I'm not stopping you.'

Emma was tempted to ask her to get out of the room, but it seemed too open to misconstruction, so she shed the towel reluctantly and quickly slipped the cream smock over her head again. Then she reached for her hairbrush, as Stacey went on:

'Jordan told me you were married. I must say, you don't act much like it. What does your husband do?'

'David?' It was difficult to sound casual, but she managed to achieve something like it. 'He—er—he's a commercial artist.'

'Really?' Stacey sounded unconvinced. 'Didn't he want to come out here with you?' She paused. 'Or wasn't he invited?'

Emma shrugged, keeping her face averted as she wielded the hairbrush. 'He—I—the Kyles have known my family for—for years. Mr Kyle—Andrew, that is—he wanted to see me, that's all, and as he'd been ill . . .'

Her voice trailed away and Stacey regarded her with narrow-eyed speculation. 'You mean because he's dying, he asked to see you?' she enquired unfeelingly, and Emma's shocked stare gave her away. 'Oh, yes, I know. Jordan and I have—known one another for some time. His frequent trips out here have not gone unnoticed.'

'I see.' Emma moved her shoulders in a dismissing gesture. 'Well, that's why I'm here.'

'How sweet!' Stacey sounded sardonic. 'And Jordan had nothing to do with it, of course.'

'Jordan?' Emma had coloured. She couldn't help it, and Stacey's lips thinned.

'Yes, Jordan,' she repeated. 'Our mutual—friend! Don't pretend you haven't noticed him.'

Emma held up her head. 'Jordan and I have known one another since we were children,' she declared tautly. 'I don't know what you're talking about.'

Stacey uttered a short mirthless laugh. 'Don't you? Since you were children, eh? What were you? Childhood sweethearts?'

'No!' Emma's face burned. 'And in any case, I don't see what our relationship has to do with you.'

'Don't you?' Stacey shrugged. 'I'm curious, that's all. As the girl Jordan's going to marry, I feel I have a right to know all his friends.'

Emma's teeth clamped together. She wanted to order the girl from the room, but to do so now would play exactly into her hands. Instead she forced herself to say politely: 'You're engaged? Congratulations! Jordan didn't tell me.'

'He wouldn't. He's not proud of the reasons why we're getting married,' retorted Stacey carelessly. 'But even a man like Jordan makes a mistake once in a while.'

Her meaning was obvious and Emma replaced the hairbrush on the dressing table with hands that trembled uncontrollably. 'A-Andrew will be pleased,' she got out jerkily. 'I imagine he would like a grandchild.'

Stacey rose gracefully from the side of the bed and surveyed her slender form in the long mirror of the wardrobe with some satisfaction. 'Do you think so?' As yet Emma could see no sign of a thickening waistline. 'Then it's up to Jordan to make it legitimate, isn't it? For all our sakes.'

Emma drew a deep breath. 'Why are you telling me this, Miss Albert?' she asked, unable to deny the question and Stacey turned patronising eyes in her direction.

'Can't you guess?' she asked maliciously. 'Because I know Jordan was in *your* bedroom last night, Mrs Ingram.'

Lunch was served in an octagonal-shaped room which

overlooked the gardens at the side of the house. Sliding glass doors were pushed open on to a patio, and beyond the mosaic paving, a kidney-shaped swimming pool was backed by a row of cabanas for changing.

The room itself was unusual, but Emma later learned that there was a matching turret at the opposite side of the building, an affectation designed by the previous owner of the property who had mistaken delusions of grandeur. Nevertheless, it was an attractive room, with walls hung with green and gold damask to match the seats of the striped Regency chairs. The table was an ellipse of polished fruit-wood, set with intricately-sewn place mats and silver cutlery, the triple-branched candelabrum indicating that dinners were sometimes served by candlelight.

A young West Indian maid served the meal of iced soup and shellfish salad, but Emma had little appetite. Because she ate so sparingly, mostly pushing the food around her plate in an effort to make it look as if she was enjoying it, she couldn't help but notice that Andrew Kyle ate little either, and even his son seemed more interested in the sheaf of letters he had brought to the table for his father's perusal than in the meal. Only Stacey consumed her food with any enthusiasm, and Emma felt a sharp pain in her stomach when she contemplated the reason for the other girl's healthy appetite. *How could he?* she was asking herself bitterly. How could Jordan have come to her bedroom last evening and made overtures of love to her when he knew that Stacey was carrying his unborn child?

From time to time she was aware of Andrew watching her, but when she lifted her head to intercept his gaze, he immediately averted his eyes. It was curious behaviour, and she wondered what he was thinking. Jordan had said he wanted her to come out here to prove there was no ill-feeling, but somehow, now she was here, that seemed a poor excuse. And yet a dying man could have strange fancies, and it was true that since her father's death there had been animosity between the families. Her mother had never blamed Andrew in any way for the crash, but then she had never appeared to like the man, despising his brashness in business, and ridiculing his accent which had altered little over the years. There were times when Emma suspected she had enjoyed baiting him, and it was natural that after all the ties with the company had been severed, she should avoid his presence. Two days ago Emma had written and told her mother what she planned to do, but she had not expected a response.

Coffee was served at the end of the meal, and Andrew suggested they had it outdoors, beside the swimming pool. There were loungers there, set on the blue and gold tiling, and a swing couch moved indolently in the slight breeze.

'Couldn't we go sailing?' demanded Stacey impatiently, as she accompanied the others outside. 'I don't want to spend the whole day lying by the pool. Jordan! *Darling!*' She looked wheedlingly up at him, tugging appealingly at his arm. 'Jordan, do say we can.'

Andrew flexed his bony shoulders. 'Yes, why don't you, Jordan?' he agreed, and the glance that passed between father and son was full of meaning: compelling on the one hand and doubtful on the other.

'And Emma?' Jordan asked tautly, holding his father's gaze, but Andrew shook his head.

'Leave Emma here,' he directed evenly. 'She can keep me company, while you and Stacey take a trip across the bay. We'll be quite content, won't we, my dear?'

'Oh! Oh, yes.' Emma's nod was urgent, and Jordan's mouth turned down at the corners.

'I don't feel like sailing this afternoon,' he declared flatly, much to Stacey's annoyance, and as if to emphasise his statement he flung himself into one of the rattan loungers. 'Maybe tomorrow,' he added, in answer to the other girl's sound of annoyance. 'Relax, Stacey. There's plenty of time.'

Andrew regarded his son with a mixture of impatience and unwilling admiration. Then, with a slight shrug, he indicated that Emma should take the lounger nearest to her, and himself relaxed into the chair beside her. Stacey, after a moment's tight-lipped fury, flounced on to the swing, and it jerked back and forward clumsily before settling into a steady rhythm.

'Isn't this nice!' remarked Jordan, but his tone was dry, and Emma wondered why he had chosen not to fall in with Stacey's wishes. What possible motive could he have for wanting to remain at the poolside, unless he, too, had his suspicions as to why his father had brought Emma out to Valentia?

There was silence for a while. Emma, glancing at Andrew, noticed that his eyes were closed, but he wasn't asleep. Even as her gaze moved past him to Jordan, his lids flickered, and in an undertone he said:

'Tell me about yourself, Emma. Tell me about your mother. Is she still living in the Lake District?'

'What?' Emma forced herself to concentrate on what he was saying. 'Oh, yes. Yes, she still lives in Cumbria.'

'Do you see much of her?'

'Not a lot, no.' Emma became aware that more than one pair of ears was listening to her conversation. 'Since—since I got married ...'

'Of course,' Andrew nodded. 'Since your marriage, you haven't had a lot of time for anything else. How is Ingram? Does he do any work?'

'Yes.' Emma coloured. 'He still gets commissions. Not so many as he used to, of course——'

'Why?' cut in Jordan at that point. 'Because you're there to support him?' His lips twisted. 'He always was a lazy devil!'

'I beg your pardon——'

'*Jordan!*' Before Emma could think of any retaliatory comment to make, his father moved to the edge of his seat, his gnarled knuckles whitening with the grip he was exerting on the arms of his chair. 'Emma is talking to me, not to you, Jordan. Why don't you go and entertain your—er—guest? We can deal quite well without your crude observations.'

Jordan, however, seemed totally unmoved by his father's anger. Stretching his booted feet towards the pool, he settled more comfortably in his chair, regarding them both through the short thick lashes that fringed his half-closed lids.

Andrew, after a moment's silent battle, gave up the fight and relaxed once more against the cushions. 'I must apologise for my son, Emma,' he exclaimed, clicking his tongue in irritation. 'He can be very trying at times.'

Jordan's mouth revealed his cynicism, and Emma endeavoured not to look his way again. Between the swaying fringes of the couch, Stacey was watching the proceedings with something akin to boredom, but when her eyes rested on Jordan, they contained more than a trace of jealous possession.

Andrew began to talk again, asking Emma more general things about her life in England, questioning her about her job with Gilda Avery, reminding her that despite the distance that separated him from Abingford, he was just as deeply interested in its affairs as ever.

The only thing he never touched on was his own health, and Emma found it impossible to ask him about his illness in Jordan's mocking presence. That he was not a well man was evident in the greyness of his features, in the faintly translucent quality of his skin; and what could she say that would not sound gratuitous?

In the late afternoon Andrew fell asleep, and only then did Jordan rise slowly to his feet, stretching with evident relief in the expansion of his muscles. Then, as Stacey swung her legs expectantly to the ground, he turned to Emma and said in a low voice:

'Would you like to swim now? In the sea, of course.'

Emma's lips parted silently, startled by his unexpected change of mood, and Stacey took the opportunity to take possession of his arm and say eagerly: 'Did you say swim? Darling, I thought you'd never ask!'

Jordan glanced at her half impatiently, then he looked at Emma again. 'Well?' he mouthed, and she pressed her lips together for a moment, unwilling to answer him. 'Come on,' he persisted. 'He's not in the glare of the sun, and he'll sleep for an hour at least.'

With a sigh, Emma got to her feet, and facing him, she murmured: 'I didn't bring a swimsuit.'

'You didn't?' Jordan's surprise was short-lived. 'No, well, I guess you wouldn't.' He turned to Stacey. 'Do you have a suit of some kind you could lend Emma?'

'I doubt if—Emma—would want to wear anything of mine,' demurred the other girl coolly. She looked squarely at her. 'Do you normally wear a bikini or a one-piece?'

Emma shook her head. 'I don't—normally—wear either,' she replied evenly. 'I don't do a lot of swimming these days.'

'Don't you?'

Jordan was looking at her and unwillingly she remembered the nights they had swum in the river, nights when wearing a swimsuit had seemed an unnecessary encumbrance ...

Tearing her eyes away, she bent her head, shaking it again vigorously. 'You—you two go,' she exclaimed tautly. 'I——'

'That's a good idea,' interposed Stacey, but Jordan wasn't listening to her.

'Go and get a swimsuit for Emma,' he said shortly, and with a venomous backward glance, she complied.

Alone with Jordan, Emma put some distance between them, but he came after her, catching her wrist and looking down at her with unconcealed impatience. 'Don't you want to come?' he demanded. 'Or is it Stacey? Did you believe what she told you?'

Emma stared at him in amazement, and his mouth took on a mocking curve. 'Voices carry,' he told her softly. 'And if you remember I was just down on the verandah.'

'But—but Stacey said you were asleep!' Emma protested, forgetting for the moment what he had heard, and he shrugged.

'Have you ever known me sleep in the morning?' he retorted. 'Except in bed, of course.'

Emma shook her head helplessly. 'You—you——'

'Will this do?'

Silently, Stacey had returned carrying two swimsuits, and Jordan's hand fell from Emma's wrist with casual indifference. The suit Stacey had chosen for the other girl was a plain pink bikini. Her own suit was two scraps of scarlet lace held together with slender white cords, and while Emma realised Stacey had chosen the contrast deliberately, she was relieved she didn't have to wear the too-brief scarlet bikini. It was barely decent, and despite, or maybe because, of her relationship with Jordan, she could not wear such a thing in front of him. Whatever had been between them had been natural and wholesome, not the result of deliberate provocation.

The girls changed in the cabanas, and it was only as she viewed her appearance in the mirror that lined one wall that Emma realised Jordan had not denied Stacey's accusation. All he had done was to ask her whether she believed it. And that could mean anything.

Outside again, the subject of her speculations was just emerging from the house again. In their absence, he had been indoors and changed into denim shorts that exposed the powerful length of his legs and revealed that his skin was used to the rays of the sun. His eyes flickered over her briefly, then he remarked dryly: 'Stacey surely didn't know what she was doing lending you that suit.'

Emma glanced down at herself in embarrassment. 'It looks all right, doesn't it? I like it.'

'So you should,' he conceded shortly, and Stacey's appearance robbed her of the necessity to think of some suitable retort.

The other girl was sufficiently satisfied with her own appearance not to pay too much attention to Emma. Slipping her arm through Jordan's, she insisted she needed his assistance to descend the cliff path, and Emma was forced to follow them at a much slower pace than she would have liked.

Shallow steps had been cut into the rock face, and there was no difficulty about the descent. The hardest thing, Emma guessed, would be to climb the steps after an exhausting hour's swimming, but she was so enchanted by her surroundings, she determinedly put all other considerations aside. There would be time enough to worry about David, and Andrew, Stacey's startling revelations, and her own futile emotions. For the present she was going to enjoy the moment ... and let it last.

The shoulders of the headland curved round this natural basin, and Jordan warned them both that the land shelved rapidly beyond the shallows. Stacey suggested they swam out to the yacht, but Jordan said it was too far for a first attempt, and they contented themselves with exploring the underwater life of the shoreline.

Emma, left to her own devices, decided she would swim to the yacht. It was not far, barely a quarter of a mile, she estimated, and the exercise would do her good. Her whole body felt tense with pent-up feelings, a sensation of thwarted excitement that was not relieved by the sight of Stacey winding her arms about Jordan's neck and pulling him under. The physical energy needed to achieve her objective might release the tension she was feeling, and leave her pleasantly exhausted.

She heard Jordan call her name once as she left them playing in the shallows, but she pretended not to hear him. She didn't want his advice or his censure. She only wanted to get away from both of them. Stacey would be pleased, she thought with a pang. She hadn't wanted her to join them in the first place.

It was further to the yacht than she had at first imagined, and her arms were aching by the time she reached the ladder that was suspended over the hull. She clung to the rungs for several seconds taking huge gulps of air, and then heard the sound of someone, or something, behind her. She glanced round just as Jordan's muscular arm reached past her to grasp the ladder, and felt the wet, slippery length of his body right behind her.

'I said it was too far to swim out here,' he grated in her ear, and she looked over his shoulder to see if Stacey had followed him.

'I didn't ask you to come after me,' she protested, when she saw that the other girl was still standing in the shallows, looking after them with what Emma was sure was malevolent hostility, but Jordan only made a sound of impatience.

'Can you climb on board?' he asked, without answering her, and she nodded before saying: 'I think so.'

It was harder than she had thought to put one foot above the other and her legs felt like jelly when she stumbled on to the deck. But she managed to pull herself along by the side of the cabin windows, and flopped in an ungainly heap on the engine housing. Jordan followed her, his shorts dripping wetly on to the shining boards, his hair several shades darker with the salt water.

Avoiding his gaze, Emma stared determinedly about her. It was a luxurious vessel, that much she could see at a glance, with a hardwood hull and bronze fastenings. Through the windows of the cabin she could see the padded cushions of the banquettes that lined the walls, and the polished wood of the table that formed a barrier between. It was obviously capable of sailing long distances, and she wondered if Jordan and his father had used it for that purpose. It made her realise how little she knew of his life these days, and reminded her anew of the differences in their financial status.

Jordan leaned against the rail that ran around the deck area, and regarded her half impatiently. Then he said quietly: 'You knew I would follow you, didn't you? Why did you do it, Emma? Wasn't last night warning enough for you?'

She scrambled to her feet at his words, and wrung the water out of her hair, leaving it to hang in an ebony rope over one shoulder. Then, squaring her shoulders, she said firmly: 'I didn't know you'd follow me. And as for—for last night, well—after what Stacey told me——'

'Oh, come on!' His temper snapped suddenly. 'You didn't believe all that, did you? I know Stacey's game, but

I'm not stupid. When I choose to marry someone, it will be on my terms, not theirs.'

Emma's lips trembled as she looked up at him. 'And—and the baby?'

'There is no baby!' declared Jordan harshly, turning to rest his elbows on the rail. 'I don't know how she's become suspicious of our relationship. I surely didn't say anything. But she was waiting for me last night when I got back from your room, and it didn't need a degree in psychology to see I was not my usual charming self!'

Emma bent her head. 'No doubt she proved an adequate substitute,' she ventured, but his angry intake of breath belied her words.

'That's some opinion you have of me, isn't it?' he said violently. 'I'm sorry to disappoint you, but I'm not an animal. Contrary to your belief, I do not find one woman as satisfactory as another!'

'So you didn't sleep with her?'

'No, I didn't sleep with her,' he agreed grimly. 'Unlike you, I have no desire to tie myself to someone I don't love.'

'But—but why didn't you say something? Why didn't you deny it?' Emma cried. 'Why did you let her get away with it?'

Jordan straightened, regarding her with disturbing intensity. 'Why should I deny something that will deny itself in the course of time? Why should I give her a reason to air her grievances in public? Because that's what she would do, I know. And you're a perfect target.'

'Me?'

'Yes, you. As you maintained so fervently last evening, you are married, and unless Andrew——'

He broke off abruptly, and Emma stared at him expectantly. 'Unless Andrew—what?' she prompted, but he shook his head, and his expression took on the cool, detached mask she was coming to know so well.

'You're cold,' he said, and his words drew her attention to the fact that she was indeed shivering, but whether that was with the cold or reaction, she couldn't be sure. 'Come down to the cabin,' he suggested, indicating the stairway that led below. 'I think my father keeps something on board to ward off chills on occasions like this.'

Emma hesitated. 'What about—Miss Albert?'

Jordan cast a resigned look shorewards. '*Miss* Albert can take care of herself,' he replied, and went ahead of her down the steps.

The twenty-two-feet-long cabin was divided into galley and living areas. The teak fittings were satin-smooth, and the warmth engendered by wall-to-wall carpeting could be dispelled, if required, by an efficient air-conditioning system. There was a bar and lounging area, and a small cabin aft which Jordan explained had two independent berths. The galley was all-electric, with a rotisserie oven and even a deep-freeze, and there was room to relax in the wheelhouse, with all-round observation.

Emma was very conscious of her wet swimsuit as she accompanied Jordan into the cabin, but he dismissed her half-formed protests. 'Here's a towel. Use it if you must,' he advised, tossing her a soft blue bathsheet from its storage place in one of the ottomans, and she wrapped its folds about her gratefully.

Apparently uncaring that he was dripping water on to the carpet, Jordan opened the bar and set two glasses aside while he unscrewed the cap of a bottle of brandy. 'Genuine Napoleon,' he declared, handing her a glass containing a generous measure. 'Guaranteed to fire the iciest blood.'

Emma took the glass reluctantly, but aware she was still shivering, in spite of the towel, she took a tentative sip. The raw spirit burned her throat and stung her eyes, but it sent the blood rushing through her veins and discernibly her skin felt warmer. The chill in her stomach was dissipating a little, too, although that was as much at the knowledge that Stacey had been lying to her as the effect of the potent liquid.

'Better?' asked Jordan, having swallowed the measure he had poured himself and replaced his glass on the bar. 'It's certainly brought some colour to your cheeks.'

'Yes, thank you.' Emma took another swallow, and gulped as it descended. 'I hope your father won't object.'

Jordan shook his head and turned to put the bottle back in its place. 'He won't.' Then he turned again, and said: 'Tell me, when I asked you to come out here, did you think it was a strange request?'

Emma quivered once more as the implications of what he was asking struck a matching chord inside her. 'I—you said your father wanted to see me. I could understand that —I think.'

Jordan's brows arched. 'But didn't you wonder why he should wait so long before—before breaching the gap?'

Emma frowned. 'Why are you asking me these things? Don't you know? You're your father's son.'

'I know that.' Jordan's mouth was tense with emotion. Then he said unexpectedly: 'Did you—did you speak to your father before he died?'

'Me? Speak to him?' Emma stared at him blankly. 'I don't understand what you mean.'

Jordan sighed, moving restively about the cabin as he sought for words. 'I mean, did you know he saw my father just before—just before—well, on the night he died?'

Emma tried to think. 'I think so. He'd been to Athelmere, hadn't he? Afterwards I thought he'd been to see your father to—to ask for help.'

Emma remembered very well her mother's bitterness at

that time. Asking Andrew Kyle for anything had been anathema to her. And besides, she knew her husband was wholly responsible for the crippling financial state of his affairs.

Now Jordan halted in front of her, staring down at her intently. 'And did your mother tell you that? That your father had asked mine for help?'

'Not in so many words, no.' Emma couldn't sustain his gaze and looked down at her hands, curved tightly round the folds of the towel. 'Why? Why are you asking?' She paused for a moment, and then as an idea occurred to her, she looked up again. 'Is that what you're trying to tell me? That—that Daddy—asked Andrew for help, and he refused? Is that why he's brought me out here? To try and assuage his conscience?'

'*No!*' Jordan's denial was harsh and angry. 'No. Never think that. What my father did, he did for the best reasons, I'm sure. He's not the kind of man to shirk his responsibilities. If you knew——'

He broke off again, and frustration sharpened her tongue. 'If I knew what? What?' she cried helplessly. 'Why do you persist in avoiding a straight answer? Is there something I ought to know? If there is, you should tell me!'

Jordan's jaw worked silently for a moment, then he said savagely: 'All right, all right. Did you know that your father borrowed money from mine? Did you know that they were private loans, not recorded in the company? That at your father's death, he owed mine something in the region of one hundred thousand pounds?'

'No!' Now it was Emma who attempted a denial, but the conviction in Jordan's face was too harsh to defend. 'He—he couldn't!' she exclaimed, withdrawing from him, sinking down on to the soft banquette and pressing her back against it. 'We—we would have known.'

'Would you?' Jordan came down on to the cushioned seat beside her, one elbow resting on its back, his other arm resting along his thigh. 'How well did you know your father, I wonder? How well does anyone know another person?'

Emma thrust her half empty glass on to the floor, unable to continue holding it in her unsteady fingers. Jordan was too close, his eyes were surveying her too intently, and unwillingly the need to plead for his sympathy was making itself felt.

'You—you think your father has brought me out here to tell me this?' she ventured faintly, and he shrugged.

'Perhaps. Among other things.'

'What other things?'

'He'll tell you what he feels you ought to know.'

'Oh, Jordan!' Helplessly, she let the towel slip aside as she stretched her hand towards his knee, her fingers closing compulsively over his thigh. 'Jordan, I'm scared.'

'Scared?' He stared at her, making no attempt to remove her hand. 'You have nothing to be scared about.'

'I do. I do!' The need to confess was on her, and she scarcely thought that the brandy, swallowed on an empty stomach, might be loosening her tongue. 'Jordan, I don't know what I'm going to do. David—David and I, we—we parted so—so hatefully. And this business over the girl, Sandra Hopkins, it—well, it's not something one can forget——'

'Do you want to forget it?' demanded Jordan, in a low husky voice, and she looked up at him tremulously.

'I—I don't know,' she admitted honestly, her tongue appearing, to moisten her upper lip. 'If—if there's to be any future for us, I'll have to, won't I?'

'Oh, *God*!' Jordan dragged his gaze away from her forcefully, even while his hand covered hers on his thigh with almost cruel pressure. 'Emma, you could stay here. Have you thought of that? Here on the island. Far away from Ingram and his damned scheming!'

'With—with you?' she tendered softly, but his rejection of that was immediate.

'Not with me, no,' he retorted, and she withdrew her hand as if his flesh had suddenly burned her. 'With my father. He—he needs you.'

'And you don't?' she countered bitterly, but he didn't react as she had expected.

'I just want you to be happy, Emma,' he insisted harshly, combing his fingers through her hair for several heart-stopping moments. 'Don't make it so hard for me.' Then he rose to his feet again. 'Come on. We'd better go back before Stacey decides she'll come after us.'

'I—I'm surprised she hasn't,' declared Emma unsteadily, folding the towel and hanging it over a radiator, evidence of the craft's capacity for sailing in colder waters.

'I'm not.' Jordan stood to allow her to precede him up the steps. 'She's not a strong swimmer. She would never tackle this distance without me.'

Emma swung over the side on to the ladder, feeling the need to get under his skin as he always succeeded in getting under hers. 'I suppose that means she—needs you,' she observed, hiding the pain she had no more right to feel than he had to inflict, and his features took on an expression of impatience.

'I thought we'd handled that,' he protested, coming after her, but she dropped into the water before he could reach her, and swam powerfully for the beach.

CHAPTER SEVEN

EMMA heard the telephone ringing during the uneasy night that followed, but it was all part and parcel of the strangeness of her surroundings. Despite the feather-soft comfort of her bed, she slept shallowly, waking at the slightest sound, aware of Stacey's room next door and an urgent desire not to know if Jordan chose to share it.

She had retired early, directly after Jordan's father had said his goodnights at ten o'clock, and deliberately closed the balcony doors so that she would not be an unwilling eavesdropper to any conversation. In consequence, the room became uncomfortably warm as the night wore on which did not help. She had shed her nightgown and slept naked, but even that was no assistance, and indeed accentuated her over-stimulated senses.

The evening had been an anti-climax, to say the least. She had returned to the house alone, leaving Jordan to make his apology to Stacey unobserved, and as Andrew was still sleeping, she had dressed in the cabana and then retreated to the comparative safety of her room. There was always the possibility that Stacey might follow her, of course, but a chair under the handle of the door would at least give her some warning, and in the event it was unnecessary. Whatever Jordan had said to his girl-friend, she had accepted his explanation, and while Emma paced restlessly about her bedroom, she could hear their voices echoing from the patio below.

Not knowing whether she ought to dress for dinner,

Emma had showered and then dressed in a midi-length gown of violet-coloured chiffon, whose flared skirt had survived the fashions since the trousseau for which it had been bought. It had not had many airings in the past four years, and still became her as well as it had ever done. With the wings of her hair curtaining her face from a central parting, she had been satisfied with her appearance, and prepared to do battle with Stacey should the need arise.

But it hadn't. Stacey had come in to dinner with Jordan, slim and attractive in a white lace trouser suit that exposed the pale skin to the harmless night air, and from the way she hung on his every word, he had successfully allayed any suspicions she might have been nurturing.

Andrew Kyle looked tired as he tackled the wine-flavoured casserole of chicken, and although Emma felt it was encumbent upon her to explain that she could not stay for more than a couple of days, she hadn't the heart to speak to him then. Instead, the meal passed without incident, and afterwards, Jordan gave in to Stacey's suggestion that he should show her a little of the island by moonlight. His invitation for Emma to join them was perfunctory, and naturally she refused, but if she had expected that Andrew might talk to her now that they were alone at last, she was disappointed. Excusing his lack of conversation, he lay back in his chair, obviously weaker than she had imagined, and as soon as Jordan returned, he retired.

When Emma awakened to daylight at last, it was already nine o'clock. Thrusting back the sheet which was all she had used to cover herself, she padded across the floor to the windows, and thrust wide the balcony doors. The house was not overlooked, so she had no fears for her nudity being observed, and the sight of the blue-green waters of the Caribbean splashing ribbons of white foam along the rocks of the headland couldn't help but give her a feeling of well-being. It was such a beautiful island, she mused helplessly. How could anyone not respond to its charm?

She was in the shower when she heard someone in the bedroom, and hastily wrapping a towel about herself, she went to investigate. She was unutterably relieved when she found not Stacey as she had half expected, but the maid who served their dinner the night before setting a tray on the table beside her bed.

'Good morning, ma'am,' she greeted her politely. 'This is your breakfast. Maggie says she hopes you don't care for an English meal.'

Emma towelled herself dry as she walked towards the maid. Really, she thought, she was getting quite brave, walking about with only a towel as covering, but she smiled at the maid and said: 'Rolls and fruit juice are fine with me. Tell Maggie I couldn't eat a cooked breakfast to save my life.'

'Yes, ma'am.' The maid smiled in return and left her, and fastening the towel sarongwise about her, Emma seated herself beside the tray.

She found she was quite hungry. Perhaps the abnormality of the events of the day before and the fact that she had not felt hungry then had something to do with it. Whatever it was, she ate all the rolls she had been given, interspersing them with the fresh orange juice and several cups of strong black coffee.

Then she dressed. She put on a pair of white cotton pants and a blue and white spotted vest, and instead of coiling her hair at her nape as she often did for working, she secured it with a white hairband and left it loose about her shoulders. Viewing her appearance in the mirror of the dressing table, she realised the casual attire made her look younger, which she wasn't at all sure was a good thing. She looked much as she had looked when she had first become aware of Jordan, and she wondered if she ought to wear a bra after all.

But it was too hot, and when she carried her tray downstairs again, she was glad she had not given in to the impulse to wear something more in keeping with her image of a young married woman. Tomorrow, or the day after, she might be on her way home, and she was not harming anybody, after all.

She encountered Maggie in the hall, and she protested that Emma needn't have bothered returning the tray, one of the maids would have collected it when the beds were made.

'It's no trouble,' declared Emma, relinquishing her burden with a smile. 'And I'm afraid I made my bed, too. I'm not used to being waited on, as no doubt you've guessed.'

Maggie shook her head. 'Most guests don't give it a thought,' she said, balancing the tray on one hip. 'Did you sleep well?'

Emma avoided a direct answer. 'The bed was very comfortable. Er—how is Mr Kyle this morning? He seemed very tired last night.'

The housekeeper nodded. 'Your arrival was too much for him, I think. He'll be better today, you'll see. He's not down yet, but when he does appear, would you like me to let you know?'

'Oh—yes. Thank you.' Emma glanced about her doubtfully. 'Am I first up?'

'No, no.' Maggie was very firm. 'Jordan was up and out two hours ago. There was a phone call early this morning —from Los Angeles. He's flown to Barbados to meet some West Coast representative of another electronics firm. He left before eight.'

'I see.' Emma felt an unwilling pang of disappointment. 'Did he—did he—er—say when he'd be back?'

'Not in so many words, no, Mrs Ingram. But I reckon he won't be away more than a day or so.'

'A day or so!' Emma licked her dry lips. 'But I—I——' She broke off, realising it was no concern of Maggie's that she might have to leave before Jordan returned. 'Thank you. Thank you for letting me know. I—er—I'll be outside if Mr Kyle wants me.'

The hall of the house was cool and spacious, but when she emerged on to the verandah at the front of the building, the sun was pouring brilliantly down through the slats of the canopy that provided oases of shade. Below the house, the lawns gave way to flowering shrub hedges and vine-hung trellises, where stalks of red and purple bougain-villea twined between the lattices, and in the distance the blue-gold haze of the ocean shimmered on the horizon.

Stepping across the lawns, she felt the heavy dew invading her sandals, and bent to smell the freshness of the earth. The air was alive with birds and insects of all kinds, and there was the steady beat of their wings as they spun past her ears. A humming-bird hovered close by and Emma stared in wonder at the palpitating flutter of its wings, marvelling at its ability to hang in the air without plummeting towards the earth.

An elderly West Indian was employed in weeding the flower gardens, but he seemed more than content to lean on his fork and watch her as she threaded her way along the paths to where a stone seat had been hewn out of a rocky outcrop, and from where there was a magnificent view of the bay. Deciding to rest for a while, she seated herself in the embrasure, and leant her head back against the sun-warmed stone.

Unwillingly, her thoughts turned to her eventual return to England—and to David. Jordan's sudden departure had alerted her awareness of how accessible Valentia really was, and no matter how remote it seemed from the problems of her marriage, it was only a phone call away. That phone she had heard ringing the night before could have been David calling her, and if he had, what would she have done about it? What *could* she have done about it?

Irresistibly, thinking of the phone message brought less controllable thoughts of Jordan and the curious relationship between them he had created. It was as though he felt obliged to treat her with a mixture of anger and respect, yet all the while she was aware of other emotions tearing that veneer aside. She didn't understand him, and she didn't understand what he expected of her. He didn't love her, not as she loved him, for it was useless to deny that her feelings for him had undergone any fundamental change over the years. They had been stifled, that was all, but now, forced in his presence, they were expanding with a complete disregard for the means of their stimulation.

She smoothed the rough stone with her finger tips and tried to think positively about the future. Sooner or later she was going to have to make a decision about David, and while she might despise him for his relationship with the other girl, nothing could alter the fact that she had married him in full knowledge of his disability. To bring up the past now was like raking over old fires, and although he had been disloyal to her, basically the situation hadn't changed. Even if Sandra had been with him when he crashed, he was still the invalid she had always known him to be, and to walk out on him now, when he obviously needed her, was not in her nature to do. And he knew it. It was easy to think now that Sandra should have married him, that she should have had the task of taking care of him all these years. *She hadn't*, and she was no doubt married now with a family of her own.

The sun was warm upon her face as she sat there,

sheltered from its direct glare; and perhaps because she had slept so badly the previous two nights, she fell asleep, and it was here that Andrew Kyle found her some forty minutes later.

'Emma!' His gentle ejaculation disturbed her slumbers, and she opened her eyes wide to find him gazing down at her with something akin to anxiety in his expression. 'Emma, my dear, are you all right?'

'Andrew!' she breathed dazedly. Then, as she remembered where she was, she straightened, saying hastily: 'Yes. Yes, I'm fine, thank you. I must have fallen asleep—I'm sorry. Have you been worried about me?'

'I've been looking for you for almost fifteen minutes,' he told her, sinking down on to the stone bench beside her. 'I didn't realise you'd found my little hideaway. Do you like it? I sit here for hours when I'm alone.'

Emma ran smoothing hands over her tumbled hair and nodded. 'It's the most perfect place,' she agreed. 'And the view . . .' She smiled. 'You're very—lucky.'

She chided herself for the faint hesitation she had shown before finishing the sentence. Andrew might not be aware of the seriousness of his condition, and her careless tongue must not alert him to her knowledge. Rushing on, she added: 'It's the ideal place to retire to, isn't it? I know I envy you. Looking out on to our rain-swept garden doesn't compare with this!'

'Doesn't it?' Andrew was watching her closely as he spoke, and only by an immense effort of will power did she prevent the revealing colour from flooding her cheeks. But seemingly it was not enough. 'Oh, Emma,' he exclaimed, tugging a strand of the dusky hair that lay on her shoulder, 'you don't have to pretend with me. I know I'm dying. I've known it for a long time. So long in fact that death and I have become quite old adversaries.'

'Andrew!'

Emma stared at him unhappily, but the man merely shook his head, no more perturbed than previously. 'It's true,' he declared gently. 'Don't look like that. I've had quite a good run for my money, longer than a lot of my friends have had. Jeremy, for instance.'

Emma bent her head, catching her upper lip between her teeth. Then she sighed. 'It doesn't seem fair somehow. My father cared so little for his life that he destroyed it, and now—now you're having yours destroyed for you.'

Andrew nodded. 'Put like that, it does sound a paradox, doesn't it? But then that's life. We can't ever know how things will turn out.'

Emma lifted her head. 'Why did you bring me out here, Andrew?' She held his gaze. 'Was it just to see the families —united? Because if so, then I think my mother——'

'No.' Andrew's brief denial interrupted her, and she broke off what she was saying to look expectantly at him. 'No,' he said again. 'It wasn't just for that, although if I had my time over again ... But there,' he seemed to shrug away the sudden depression that had gripped him, 'we can't change our lives no matter how we try. We're all trapped within the scheme of things, flapping about like birds in a net trying to make their escape. I see my life like that— a series of foolish mistakes, that viewed objectively seem so—so futile.'

Emma listened to him with some misgivings. What was Andrew about to tell her? That her father had asked him for money and he had refused it? Was he about to take the blame for her father's suicide? Knowing what Jordan had told her, she couldn't allow that.

'Andrew ...' she began, but he raised his hand to silence her.

'No, Emma,' he said. 'Let me go on. It's little enough I

can do for you now, but I must tell you about—about your father. I wouldn't if I thought it was going to cause you any unhappiness, but I feel you have the right to know the truth.'

'What truth?' Emma moved her shoulders helplessly. 'Andrew, if it's about the money——'

'Money? What money?' Andrew stared at her blankly.

'The money ...' Emma found it difficult to go on. 'Andrew, I know Daddy owed you money when—when he died.'

Andrew's brows drew together. 'How do you know that? There was no documentation.'

Emma sighed. 'Oh—oh, does it matter? If that's what you have to tell me——'

'It's not.' Andrew was adamant. 'And I can guess how you found out. It was Jordan, wasn't it? But then Jordan always thought your mother got off too easily.'

'My mother?' Emma shook her head. 'What do you mean?'

'It's a long story ...' And already Andrew was looking weary.

'Andrew, do you think——'

'It's something I have to do,' he stated definitely. 'Now, where should I start? I suppose the beginning is the best place.'

Settling his bony shoulders back against the sun-warmed rock-face, he rested his hands on his knees before saying: 'I first met your mother in 1951.'

'In 1951?' echoed Emma in surprise. 'But that was before she and Daddy were married!'

'That's right,' Andrew nodded. 'Do you remember the Exhibition? The Festival of Britain, as it was called? I met her there, one windy July afternoon.'

'I don't remember it. I've heard of it, of course.'

'Of course.' Andrew sighed. 'Well, I was working for an electrical engineering firm in those days. It was just a small company, and later, when the owner died, he left the business to me. It was just a small company, nothing like Trace Transmissions at that time, but it was through selling that company that I had the money to buy into your father's business later.'

'I see.' Emma didn't quite see what this had to do with her, but she couldn't deny the shock she had felt upon learning that he had known her mother before her marriage. She had always maintained she despised the man, and the relationship between the two families had only been cemented by the friendship of the two men, and Emma's growing relationship with Jordan.

'Anyway,' he went on, 'we—your mother and I—were what you might call—attracted to one another.'

'You and Mummy!'

The amazement in her voice got through to him and he smiled rather wryly. 'That's right,' he said. 'Me—and your mother. Oh, it didn't last. She was already engaged to your father, and you know she always considered I wasn't good enough for her——'

'Oh, no!'

'Oh, yes,' he nodded. 'I used to resent that, bitterly. But perhaps it was a kind of defence. Even after we were married to our respective partners, we were still aware of one another, and given half a chance, I'd probably have wrecked my marriage for her.'

'You would?'

Emma was incredulous, but he only laughed, albeit a little wryly. 'Yes. Foolish, wasn't it? But there you are. I was young then, and not unlike Jordan is today.'

Looking at him, Emma could see what he meant. They were alike, and in his youth Andrew must have attracted women just as his son did now.

'So ...' Andrew crossed his legs and linked his fingers round them. 'You know the situation. Maybe you'll remember the circumstances after I tell you what happened.' He paused. 'Can we be the arbiters of our own destinies? Maybe if Jeremy had had more confidence in himself, he would never have believed what I told him.'

Emma frowned. 'What—what you told Daddy? What did you tell him?'

Andrew stared broodingly towards the headland. 'I told him you were my child—my daughter. I said your mother had been pregnant at the time of her marriage to him!'

For several minutes after he had finished speaking there was complete silence. Emma dragged her gaze away from him to stare in blank disbelief into the middle distance while the horrifying implications of what he had said created havoc in her mind, and Andrew himself seemed exhausted by the admission. A thousand and one objections to his statement were flooding her brain, not least her own abortive love for Jordan, and the possibility that her parents, and most particularly her mother, might have lied to her all these years was more than she could absorb.

'But—but am I—I'm not——'

'No, you're not,' he stated weakly, halting her babbling protests. 'You're your father's daughter. There was never any doubt.'

Emma was shaking so much she could hardly sit still. 'But—but why—how——'

'I'll explain.' He closed his eyes as if the effort was rapidly becoming too much for him. 'It is true that—that your mother and I were more than just good friends. But that was all over weeks before her wedding——'

'Then how could Daddy——'

'Let me finish.' He opened his eyes again. 'First, let me

at least try and explain how it happened. *Why* it happened. I'll never forget that night as long as I live, and nor, I suspect, will your mother.'

'My mother!'

'Oh, yes. She was there. She heard what I had to say. And the most damnable thing was—she couldn't deny our relationship. I think it was that as much as anything that caused him to believe me. Oh, yes'—this as Emma would have broken in on him, 'yes—I have a lot to answer for, I know. It hasn't been easy for me, though. My conscience has never let me forget——'

'Your conscience.' Emma almost spat the words at him. 'Oh, my God! How could you?'

'A man scorned is much the same as a woman, Emma,' he replied quietly. 'You're young. Perhaps you haven't yet learned that no one is all bad or all good. We all have our faults——'

'But to tell him—*that*!' Emma felt sick. 'Didn't my mother deny it?'

'Of course she did. But you haven't let me finish. You know now—thanks to Jordan's carelessness—that your father had borrowed money from me. Your mother didn't know that. Not until—that night. Jeremy had come to ask for another loan, and I refused it. When your mother came looking for him, he told her he was finished, that he was in debt—and I wouldn't help him.' He shook his head wearily. 'He'd been drinking. Looking back on it now, I don't think he really knew what he was doing. But when your mother turned on me—berating me, ridiculing me, telling me that if it hadn't been for Jeremy I wouldn't have been where I was today, I think I lost my head.' He pressed a hand to his chest as if it pained him, and then went on: 'I don't know why I said it. I don't know what put it into my

head. I guess I wanted to hurt your mother—but it back-
fired.'

Emma was shaking with emotion. 'And—and Mummy
denied it?'

'Yes, yes. But Jeremy wouldn't listen. It was all part and
parcel with the failure he believed himself to be.'

Emma got to her feet then, unable to sit any longer under
the strain of her emotions. She took a few tentative steps
across the grass and then turned, her face pale and drawn.
'So—so that was why——'

'Why? Why what?'

'Why Jordan walked out on me, of course.'

'No!' Andrew denied it vigorously. 'How could it be?
He never knew. How could he? It was between the three of
us. Besides,' his brows drew together, 'he told me—you'd
walked out on him. Naturally, I thought—your mother——'

'No!' Emma caught her breath on a choking gasp. For a
few moments, no matter how futile it had proved to be, she
had believed she had found the reason for Jordan's denial
of his love for her. Now it seemed he had lied to his father,
just as he had lied to her.

'I'm sorry.' It was inadequate recompense for the trauma
he had caused her and he knew it. 'Emma, you do understand why——'

'Why you had to tell me? Yes. To expunge your conscience!'

Her tone was bitter and suddenly he looked unutterably
worn. 'I'm not a religious man, Emma. If I was, I could have
made my confession to a priest and gained absolution. But
I'm not—and I felt you had the right to know why your
mother would never accept any help from me—after ...'

Emma moved her shoulders. 'I don't know what to
think.'

Andrew sighed. 'I know I can't ask you to forgive me.'

'To forgive you?' Emma made a negative gesture. 'It's too soon. I can't even take it in.'

'I understand that. It must be a great shock to you. I shall even understand if you feel you hate me. Believe me, it's no more than I hate myself. Than your mother has hated me all these years!'

Emma scuffed her toe against the warm earth. 'I can't stay here,' she said, the words almost inaudible. 'I have to go now. I have to leave——'

'Why?'

'Why?' She stared at him. 'Why do you think?'

'Because you can't bear to be in the same house as me, to eat at the same table, to sleep under the same roof?'

'It's more than that,' she choked. 'You don't want me here. You only brought me to escape the pangs of your own conscience. Now that you've told me, I can go. Just having me here must be a constant source of irritation to you.'

'No. No, you're wrong!' Swaying a little, he rose to his feet. 'Emma, my child, you're wrong. It does me good to see you here, to have you with me. Don't you remember? Don't you remember the old days? We were friends, good friends! You were more like a daughter to——' he broke off as emotion coloured his tones. 'My dear, stay as long as you like—as long as you can. All I have left now is—friendship, affection, I hope—understanding. Don't deny me these few luxuries, even if you can never forget the terrible mistakes I've made.'

Emma shook her head. 'I don't know ...'

'You wouldn't let—Jordan drive you away, would you?' he pressed. 'My dear, I lost everything when Jeremy died —my best friend, my peace of mind, my self-respect! Your break-up with Jordan was the last straw. Naturally, I thought your mother had had a hand in that, too.'

'Mummy? No. Of course, she assured me it was for the best, but I didn't believe her.'

Andrew sighed. 'What a tangled coil! If only—but it's too late, much too late. I know. I've always known. But I had to try and escape eternal damnation.'

'Oh, Andrew!'

Looking at him, it was all too much for her. How could she summon hatred for a man she had always regarded with affection and respect? How could she condemn him when what he had said in the heat of the moment had rebounded on him, just as much as on the rest of them? Her father had been a disturbed man. Who knew what thoughts he had nurtured before he died? Andrew had suffered for eight years, and now he was dying. How could she create a vendetta with a man who had only a few short months to live?

'Give me time,' she begged in a choked voice, taking hold of one of his abnormally cold hands and squeezing it. 'Give me time!'

'And you won't leave?'

'Not today anyway,' she promised tautly, and turned away from the tears she saw in his eyes.

CHAPTER EIGHT

LUNCH was served at one o'clock, as it had been the day before, but for Emma there was a certain unreality about the whole proceedings. Even the revelations Andrew had made that morning seemed all one with her feelings of standing outside herself and watching what happened with an abnormal sense of detachment. Nothing seemed to touch her, and it was only when Stacey related some personal anecdote about Jordan that would have scraped a nerve the day before that she realised emotionally she was numb.

Her lack of reaction did not go unnoticed, however. The other girl's eyes lingered speculatively upon her pale features, and as soon as the meal was over and Andrew had departed apologetically for his own quarters, she cornered Emma as she would have slipped away to her room.

'What's going on?' she demanded, slim and golden in a tawny-coloured tunic that exposed most of her slender legs. She wasn't as tall as the other girl, but the heels she invariably wore minimised the difference, and Emma in sandals was almost on eye-level terms.

Now Emma pushed her hands into the hip pockets of her pants and faced her resignedly. 'What do you mean?' she countered. 'I was going to my room, that's all. Nothing to get alarmed about.'

'Don't patronise me!' Stacey was angry. 'I'm not alarmed. But I'd have to be a mute or a moron not to know that something's happened.' She put her hands on her

128

hips. 'Did you tell Jordan what I told you? Did you tell his father?'

Emma's relief was almost palpable. For a few awful moments, she had wondered if somehow Stacey had overheard her conversation with Andrew. But it seemed all the other girl was concerned about was that her relationship with Jordan should not be disrupted.

Moving her slim shoulders, she answered honestly: 'Why would I do that? I thought Jordan already knew.'

The faintest hint of colour darkened Stacey's cheeks. 'Well—yes. Yes, he does. I only meant ...' She sought for words with evident difficulty. 'That is—I don't want you telling tales about me to anyone,' she paused. 'Just because I chose to confide in you——'

'To confide in me?' Emma couldn't let her get away with that. 'You made your reasons for telling me perfectly clear, Miss Albert, and confidence had nothing to do with it.'

'Well, all right,' Stacey sniffed. 'Perhaps I was a little— aggressive. But surely I have a right to be.'

Emma shook her head. She didn't want to talk about it any more. The longer she remained here with Stacey, the more she became aware of the fragility of the shell shock had cloaked about her, and slowly but surely her blood was beginning to thaw. It was like coming round from an anaesthetic, she thought raggedly. First the feeling of indifference, of not caring what was happening; then the sharp pain of the scars that hadn't healed.

The sound of a car being driven up the slope towards the house was at once a relief and an anxiety. A relief, because it was a reason to escape any more of Stacey's questions; an anxiety, because who else but Jordan was likely to come to the house?

'Jordan?' Stacey's thoughts were obviously running

along similar lines. 'But I understand he'd gone to Barbados.'

'He has—he *had*!' Emma made a helpless gesture. 'Perhaps he's back.'

Their doubts were clarified a few moments later when a young maid came to find them, followed by a tall, dark-haired young men whom Emma, at least, had never seen before.

'Clive!' Stacey apparently knew his identity. 'Clive, what a lovely surprise!'

'Hello, Stacey!' He took the two hands she held out to him and squeezed them tightly. 'As soon as Jordan told me you were here, I high-tailed it right over.'

'You've seen Jordan?'

Stacey sounded surprised, and the young man explained: 'I met him this morning, at the airport. Just got back myself, actually, and when he told me he was having to go to Bridgetown and leave you here on your own—or not quite on your own ...'

His eyes had shifted to Emma standing rather awkwardly in the background, and she gave a half smile of embarrassment. Stacey, realising she had to perform an introduction, made a little gesture of indifference.

'Oh—this is Mrs Ingram,' she said, stressing the designation. 'She's—er—a friend of Jordan's father.'

'Hello, *Mrs* Ingram.' The mocking way he said her name revealed that he was not deceived by the other girl's attempted dismissal. 'As Stacey has chosen not to introduce us properly, I'll introduce myself. I'm Clive Franklin. I live here on the island, too.'

The name was faintly familiar, but Emma didn't probe it too closely as he shook her hand, aware that he held on to it longer than was absolutely necessary. He was obviously very sure of himself, and of his welcome, and she didn't altogether care for his casual assumption that she would find him as attractive as Stacey obviously did. He was handsome, of course. She had to grant him that. And no doubt he had been spoiled by a procession of women who had told him so. But his even good looks and rather flashy way of dressing didn't appeal to her, and she wondered whether Jordan would approve of him coming here in his absence.

'If you'll excuse me ...' she murmured, when she could get her hand free, but although Stacey was more than willing, Clive Franklin chose to be awkward.

'Oh, come on, *Mrs* Ingram, you're not leaving us, are you? I want to hear how old Andrew comes to have such an attractive girl-friend. And a married one, at that. Or are you a widow, Mrs Ingram? Do stay, and tell me all about yourself.'

'Clive!'

Stacey's impatient exclamation echoed Emma's instinctive withdrawal, and she left them determinedly to their own particular brand of word-play. She had met men like Clive Franklin before. London was full of them. But their immature overtures had always left her cold.

She was too restless to stay in her room, however, and presently she shed her pants and vest and wrapped a yellow cotton skirt about her waist over the swimsuit Stacey had lent her. Then, slipping out of the front of the house, she circled the pool area where she guessed Stacey was entertaining her guest, and made her way down to the beach. The yacht beckoned, rocking lazily on its anchor, and on impulse she shed the skirt and plunged into the creaming waves.

If anything it seemed further to the yacht today than it had the day before. There seemed to be a current running against her, although she realised it was only her own weakness, and just as she reached the hanging ladder she felt the stabbing pain of cramp in her left leg. It was agonising, and with dismay she realised that if it had happened moments sooner, she might not have made the yacht at all. As it was, she had to rest there for several minutes before she could summon the strength to climb on board, and even then it was a painful experience.

Collapsing on to the sun-warmed deck, she refused to think about the swim back. It was all very well telling herself that if she rested for a while she would make it, but what if she couldn't? Jordan wasn't here to come after her, and he himself had said that Stacey would never have the courage to make the trip.

It was then she thought of Clive Franklin. He probably hadn't come prepared to go swimming, but he could easily borrow some trunks of Jordan's. But how was she to attract his attention? Besides, she had virtually snubbed him. Why should he help her?

As if the thought was father to the deed, it was then that she heard the voices, drifting distantly across the water; Stacey's girlish giggles and a man's deeper laughter. She turned on to her knees and looked towards the shore, relief welling up inside her, half rising to raise her arm in a beckoning wave.

Stacey was running across the sand, her scarlet swimsuit unmistakable even from this distance, and Clive was chasing her, wearing either a pair of his own shorts or some borrowed from Jordan. But even as Emma opened her mouth to shout to them Clive caught his prey and what happened next stifled the cry in her throat. Stacey turned to him and when his arms closed about her, they sank down together on to the sand.

Emma didn't watch any more. She had seen enough. It wasn't necessary to see what happened after Clive covered the blonde girl's body with his own. The subsidence of Stacey's gurgling laughter was enough, the pregnant silence that was deafening to Emma's ears. How could she shout to them now? How could she reveal her presence when to do so would embarrass all of them? She would have to wait until they had gone and then tackle the swim alone.

When she judged it was safe to do so, she crawled along the deck and made her way down to the cabin. In spite of the heat, she was chilled, and she rescued the towel from the radiator where she had left it the day before and rubbed herself briskly.

Feeling a little warmer, both inside and out, she ventured into the galley and examined the contents of the cupboards. There was a fair supply of tinned food, and she reflected dryly that if she was marooned here, at least she wouldn't starve. There was even water in the storage tanks, and although it was inclined to be warm, too, it was drinkable. The kettle didn't work when she plugged it in, however, risking making herself a cup of coffee, and she guessed there was a master switch which had been thrown before the yacht was anchored. Instead, she satisfied herself with a can of Coke, and feeling surprisingly hungry, she opened a packet of biscuits.

Afterwards, she went back into the main cabin, and after spreading the towel over the cushions for protection, she stretched her length on one of the banquettes. It was almost pleasant lying there, feeling the rise and fall of the yacht on the faint swell, the sucking sound the water made as it ran along the bows. Or it would have been if she had had pleasanter thoughts to keep her company, her own problems briefly obscured by the shadows of Jordan's. Did he know the kind of girl Stacey was? Was he aware of her relationship with this man, Clive Franklin? Or didn't he care, so long as he had the same kind of freedom? She wished she had remained in the ignorance of her own room.

She must have fallen asleep, because when she opened her eyes again it was dark beyond the narrow windows of the saloon. Dismay brought her upright with a distinct disregard for the suddenness of her awakening, and a wave of dizziness swept over her, compounded by the empty feeling inside her. What time was it? How long had she slept? Had she been missed, and if she had, had anyone started looking for her? She hoped Andrew was not worried about her. After this morning, he would be sure to think the worst.

As soon as the nauseating dizziness subsided, she scrambled off the banquette, and just as she did so, a shaft of light swept round the cabin. It startled her so much that for a minute she couldn't speak, but then she realised that the light was not some spectre of her imagination, but a powerful torch being projected over the beam. And as she registered this, she heard voices, men's voices, and guessed that it was this that had awakened her so abruptly.

Tripping over the ends of the towel which she had pulled off the couch as she rose, she stumbled towards the stairway, calling: 'I'm here. I'm here! Who is it? Are you looking for me?'

There was silence for a moment, then she heard Jordan's harsh tones: 'Emma! For God's sake, Emma, is that you?'

'Yes, yes ...' She came out on deck, blinking in the light from their torches, just as Jordan swung himself over the side. He had not swum out to the yacht. He was fully dressed, still in the dark business suit he must have worn to go to Barbados, and she shook her head incoherently, hardly able to articulate her relief.

'Emma!' he said again, more angrily this time, and then: 'My God, haven't you heard us calling you?'

'I—no—I must have fallen asleep——' she got out nervously, but as if her unsteady words were a source of irritation to him, he interrupted her savagely, saying:

'Asleep! You've been asleep! Good God, I thought you were dead!'

'*Dead*——'

'Yes, dead!' he muttered, his hands clenched tightly at his sides, as if he dare not touch her for fear he might do her some injury. 'We found your skirt on the beach half an hour ago. What else were we supposed to think?'

'I'm sorry ...' She put out a hand appealingly. 'I—I——'

'You're *sorry*!' he snapped. 'Sorry's not enough. God, I've been half out of my mind!'

Emma began to shiver as the night air got to her, and awareness of her scarcely-clad figure caused him to tear off his jacket and toss it to her.

'Put that on!' he commanded grimly, glancing round at the small motor boat which had brought him, and its black-skinned pilot. 'We'd better get you back before my father collapses completely. Didn't you care that your carelessness might kill him? Or hasn't what he told you moved you at all? I guess you're more like your mother than I thought.'

Emma moved then, stumbling across the deck to climb down the ladder, ignoring the hand he offered to help her. 'What do you know about it?' she demanded chokingly, subsiding into the motor boat. 'Did your father discuss our conversation with you? Now that he's aired the burden of his guilt, doesn't he care who knows about it?'

'I'm his son,' retorted Jordan, dropping down into the craft beside her, and nodding to the pilot to get underweigh. 'I only know that when I came back an hour ago, he was frantic with worry about you.'

'I've said I'm sorry,' she whispered, burying her chin in the lapels of his jacket, overwhelmingly aware of its warmth, redolent with the clean male smell of his body.

'Yes, you have,' he agreed. 'But you haven't explained why you felt the need to sleep out there, or why you didn't swim back.'

'I—I——' Emma's eyes moved to the pilot, and then back to their downcast evasion. 'I got cramp, swimming out to the yacht. I was—afraid to swim back.'

'For God's sake, when did you swim out there? Stacey told me that she and Clive were on the beach all afternoon. They didn't see you, and that was why we didn't immediately suspect where you'd gone. But then William found your skirt on the beach, and—here we are.' He shook his head. 'Can you imagine my father's feelings when he saw that skirt? After what—Jeremy Trace did?'

Emma quivered. 'He thought—that I might have— have——' She broke off. 'Like my father.'

Jordan's lips twisted. 'Don't you mean—like *Jeremy Trace*?' he demanded savagely, and turned away from her.

Emma was still probing his words when the motor boat grounded on the coral sand. Without giving her a chance to argue with him, Jordan swung her out of the boat and on to the sand with little ceremony, and she was left to stumble after him in the darkness as he made his sure way to the steps. She had come down barefoot without mishap, but going up again, and in the dark, was a vastly different proposition. Pebbles made her wince, and once her toe encountered something soft and slimy, that made her shudder.

The house was a dazzling mass of lights. A comprehensive search was apparently in operation, and Jordan's call: 'I've found her!' as he entered the house was obviously intended for more ears than Maggie's, hovering expectantly in the hall.

'Oh, Mrs Ingram!' the housekeeper exclaimed, with evident relief. 'Where have you been? We've looked everywhere for you.'

'I'm sorry——'

'She was on the yacht,' put in Jordan, before Emma could explain, and then gestured that she should follow him up the stairs.

Andrew Kyle's apartments were in the west wing, incorporating the turret room over the dining room below. But Emma had little chance to absorb the decorative comfort of the apartments, before Jordan pushed her before him into the huge bedroom, where his father was lying wearily among a pile of lace-edged pillows.

'She's here!' he declared unnecessarily, as Andrew's eyes flickered over the girl he was compelling towards the bed, and his father pushed himself up on his elbows and surveyed her with undisguised relief.

'Emma!' he spoke her name weakly. 'Oh, Emma, thank God!'

As Emma made some attempt to speak, her nerves shredded by Jordan's anger, her embarrassment at how she must appear wearing only Stacey's bikini and his son's jacket almost overwhelming her, Jordan bit out the facts tersely.

'She was on the yacht,' he declared. 'She must have swum out there before Stacey and Clive went down to the beach. She says she fell asleep.'

'My dear.' Andrew held out his hand towards her. 'Are you all right? You're not ill or—or anything?'

'No. I—er——' Emma glanced uncomfortably towards

Jordan. 'I—got cramp. I was afraid to swim back.'

'Why didn't you get Clive to swim back with you?' asked Jordan shortly, overriding his father's gentle acceptance of her explanation, and she was tempted to tell him exactly why she hadn't been able to attract Clive's attention.

But instead, she murmured: 'I—I must have fallen asleep before—before they came down to the beach. I'm sorry. There's nothing more I can say.'

Andrew was nodding understandingly, grimacing at Jordan when he would have questioned her further. 'Leave it,' he exclaimed, a little of his old authority colouring his voice. 'Can't you see the child's exhausted? Go along, my dear. Go and have a warm bath. You feel chilled to the bone. I'm feeling—a little tired, so I'll see you again in the morning.'

'Very well.' Emma turned towards the door. Then she halted, albeit a little uncertainly. 'I—I really am sorry, you know. I wouldn't have—I wouldn't have done this—deliberately, you know that.'

'I know,' agreed Andrew tiredly, sinking back against the pillows, and nodding, she left them.

But in her room, she found her thoughts returning irresistibly to what Jordan had said—to many of the things he had said since they left England. That morning, when Andrew had decreed that there was no way that Jordan could possibly believe she was his father's daughter, she had accepted his word without question. Why shouldn't she? It had been such a fantastic thing to have said, and in any case, Jordan had not been involved. But suddenly, after their conversation on the boat, other remarks he had made stood out in bright relief. It seemed incredible now, with this new knowledge, that she should not have suspected his insistence that he could only care for her as a *sister*, that his love for her had undergone a fundamental change.

Maybe, like her father before her, her own lack of confidence had added conviction to the belief that Jordan had only cared for the company, and she had been easily persuaded that he had never really loved her at all.

There still remained the puzzle of how Jordan could have been so misled. Who would do such a thing? His father? No. His mother? Unlikely. Who, then? Gilda? Her stomach contracted. How could that be?

She stepped out of the bath to find she was trembling. Her knees were almost knocking from the effort of supporting her body, and she knew no amount of soul-searching could displace the wholly selfish relief she felt at discovering what must surely be the truth. Somehow Jordan had heard the lie, and believed it, and all the time since then they had both been living it. Oh, Jordan, she breathed achingly. What a waste! What a terrible waste!

But the impulse to go to him and explode the myth was quickly controlled. What useful purpose could be served by raking up the past? By eliminating the obstacles between them, she could only make the situation more unbearable, and it was easier to keep the doubt alive. So long as Jordan believed there could never be anything between them, her marriage stood a chance, and in spite of everything, she was David's wife. She was not the sort of girl to walk out on her responsibilities, and after what she had learned here, his involvement with the Hopkins girl seemed a paltry deception.

All the same, it took all her strength and determination to go down to dinner that evening as if nothing had happened. As Andrew wasn't joining them, she half wondered if Clive Franklin had been invited to stay for dinner, but in that she was mistaken. Only Jordan, Stacey and herself gathered round the table in the dining room, where half a dozen candles provided the only illumination, their flames curling slightly in the draught.

Stacey, in a clinging black dress of silk jersey crêpe, regarded Emma with hostility combined with a certain wary speculation. Obviously she wasn't altogether sold on Jordan's explanation of the other girl falling asleep on the yacht, and no doubt she was alarmed that Emma might have been an unwilling voyeur to what happened between herself and Clive Franklin. Stacey still regarded her as a rival, and even though she might have no worries on that score, Emma hated the thought of her deceiving Jordan. Not that she would say anything, Emma acknowledged, rolling a sliver of chicken round her tongue. She was no better, she thought bitterly, even though her love for Jordan could not be compared to the promiscuous tumblings of a provocative woman.

Jordan spoke little throughout the meal, reserving his comments for the food, his face darkly brooding above the rich maroon velvet of his dinner jacket. Stacey did her best to arouse his interest, but from time to time her eyes flashed in Emma's direction, as if she suspected she had already said more than she should.

When the meal was over, Emma left the table to walk out on to the patio, lifting her shoulders in helpless supplication to the beauty of the night. One could become attached to this place, she thought wistfully, listening to the raucous sounds of the tree frogs, the continual scraping of the crickets. The air had a petal softness, like the brush of silk, and the scent of magnolia and the ubiquitous woodbine drifted irresistibly about her.

'Darling, Clive's giving a party this evening,' she heard Stacy telling Jordan in a low wheedling tone. 'Couldn't we go? Your father's all right now, and—she's here.'

Emma guessed she was gesturing in her direction, and determinedly moved a little nearer to the pool. Let them go to Clive Franklin's, she thought tautly. The way they chose to run their lives was not her concern, and tomorrow, or the day after, she would be returning to England.

Jordan's reply must have been in the negative, because presently Emma heard Stacey's voice raised in protest and the unmistakable sound of her high heels clattering across the wood-blocked floor as she made her furious exit.

There was a stillness after that. Only the call of a night hawk rose above the constant chorus of the insects, soaring away into the night sky with a supreme disregard for earthbound humans. Emma wrapped her arms about herself, her fingers closing over the flesh of her upper arms, and started violently when Jordan's voice right behind her observed quietly: 'I suppose he told you.'

'I—what—who——' Emma jerked away from him abruptly, tightening her arms around her middle. 'That is —I don't know what you mean.'

'Oh, come on ...' Jordan's hands were balled in the pockets of his jacket, but even in the half light it was possible to see the way they stiffened at her words. Then, as if forcing himself to relax, he said: 'My father. I suppose he made his confession. That is why he invited you out here, isn't it? I didn't immediately grasp the import of it, but I see now. He wanted to make the situation clear before you came into your inheritance.'

'Before I what?' Emma stared at him aghast. 'I don't know what you're talking about. What inheritance?'

Jordan hunched his shoulders, and she could tell from his expression that he thought she was only playing for time. But apparently he was prepared to play along with her, and disciplining his features, he explained:

'The company—Tryle Transmissions. Don't pretend you don't know that—*he*—intends you should have half of everything when he dies——'

'*No!*' Emma was horrified. 'I'm not pretending. I don't know. How could I? It—it's not true!'

'Of course it's true. I've even been involved with the drawing up of the papers.'

'No!' She stared at him as if she couldn't believe her ears. 'No, no! You must stop it!'

'Why? It's the least he can do, I should have thought. Even if it is the cruellest cut of all. Condemning you and me to seeing one another regularly for the rest of our lives——'

'No!' Emma gazed at him in dismay. It couldn't be true. Andrew wouldn't do this, would he? And yet—and yet it was exactly what he might do. After all, he had no inkling that Jordan knew, or thought he knew, of their relationship. So far as he was concerned, he was simply making amends for the wrong he felt he had done in the past.

'What's wrong?' Jordan's lips twisted bitterly. 'You're fortunate. You've had eight years of sublime innocence, while I—while I——' He broke off emotively. 'Dear God, Emma, can you understand now ...'

She put a trembling hand to her head, unable to think of anything just then but Jordan and his need to be told the truth. Yet how could she? she argued silently. If she blurted it out now, there would be no more peace for any of them. Better the devil he knew, she thought with anguish. Better the pain of ignorance than the torment of remorse.

Clearing her throat, she said: 'I don't want your—your money, Jordan. Yours or—or your father's. When I leave here, I won't be seeing you again. You—you have your life, and I have mine. And I don't want the—the responsibility of what—what you're offering me.'

'It's not me who's offering it, Emma,' he declared harshly. 'Tell—*him*—if you have any complaints. Not me.

The will's made. I can't alter it.'

Emma shifted restively. 'But you must! Jordan, believe me! I don't want anything from—from you.'

'Is it so distasteful to you?' he demanded, bitterness carving deep lines beside his mouth. 'Has that narrow little mind of yours been shocked to the core by the realisation of human weakness—*my* weakness—for you?'

'No. No!' She put out her hand blindly, warding him off, desperate to keep him away from her, in case his need overcame her own. But he grasped her fingers and raised them to his lips, and at the touch of his mouth reason almost deserted her.

Somehow she dragged her hand away from him, and cradling it against her, she hurried across the patio and into the house. And she knew as she did so that so far as Jordan was concerned, she was closing the door on any further contact between them.

CHAPTER NINE

EMMA returned to her job at Avery Antiques exactly a week later. She had needed a couple of days after she got home to recover from the jet-lag, but she was young and healthy, and in spite of her emotional upheaval, she was eager to get back to work.

She had flown home alone. The day after her encounter with Jordan on the patio, she had told Andrew she was leaving, and although he was obviously disappointed, he put no obstacle in her path. He couldn't know of her desire to put as many miles as was humanly possible between herself and Jordan, of course, but he thought he understood her need to return to familiar surroundings. Emma did not disabuse him. He had lived in ignorance of Jordan's belief all these years. It was better he died without discovering he had destroyed their lives as well as his own.

Jordan, for his part, had offered to fly home with her, but had accepted her insistence that she could manage alone without question. Like his father, he thought he understood her motives, and it was a poignant moment when he wished her luck for the future. She knew what a terrible strain it must have been for him, behaving in the cool detached manner he had adopted in her presence. But he carried it off magnificently, and with Stacey clinging to his arm, he waved goodbye to her as the Cessna made its take-off.

Because she had let no one know when she was returning, London Airport was cold and unfriendly. The overnight flight had left her feeling strangely disorientated, and on impulse she took a taxi into London to avoid the curious stares of other commuters on the underground.

She managed to get a connection to Abingford just before lunch and dozed spasmodically as the train threaded its way through the rain-swept Buckinghamshire countryside. She wasn't hungry. The continental breakfast they had served on the plane just before landing had really been surplus to requirements, a gentle reminder of the changing time zones, and to think of eating lunch when all she really wanted to do was sleep was anathema to her.

Abingford was cold, but blessedly familiar. Handing in her ticket, and emerging into the station yard, Emma was made forcibly aware of being back on her home ground when one of Gilda's regular customers hailed her. Mr Peabody was an obsessive collector of snuff boxes, and hardly a month went by without him arriving to examine the latest items Gilda had in stock. He told her he had been attending an auction the previous day in London, and when Emma wearily began to explain why she was rather tired, he insisted on getting a taxi for her, and helping her to stow her case.

Mellor Terrace looked much the same as usual, and after paying the driver, Emma mounted the steps to Number 17 with lowering spirits. It was all very well telling herself that this was where she belonged, that David needed her; and quite another to contemplate his reactions to her after a week's absence. They had hardly parted on the best of terms, and the memory of the blow he had struck her was still there like an open sore that refused to heal. There was no evidence of it now, of course, and no doubt his mother would never believe her son could have done such a thing. But he had, and she wouldn't have been human if she hadn't felt some trepidation as she inserted her key in the lock.

There was no one about as she walked the length of the hall, and turning into the drawing room, she dumped her case on the threshold and looked thoughtfully about her. Mrs Ingram had done little in the way of housework in her absence. There was a film of dust covering polished surfaces, and the ashes of the previous night's fire still lay in the grate.

It would have been easy then to give in to the tears that irresistibly burned at the backs of her eyes, but she knew emotionalism was not what was needed. This was her home. She had left it. It was up to her to restore it to order.

But where was David—and his mother? She went out into the hall again and called: 'David, I'm home!' Her voice echoed hollowly up the stairs and, shedding her coat, she picked up her case again and carried it up to her bedroom.

Mrs Ingram had apparently been sleeping in her bed. The older woman's belongings were strewn haphazardly over chair and dressing table, and a film of the powder she invariably used was spilt on the rug beside the bed.

Refusing to allow herself to feel any indignation that David's mother should have chosen to use her room instead of one of the others, Emma carried her case out of that room again and entered the larger of the spare rooms, putting her case down on the divan, and opening it with controlled movements. She extracted the soiled garments and carried them into the bathroom, dopping them into an already overflowing linen basket, and then went downstairs again.

She was making herself a cup of tea in the kitchen when the front door opened and David and his mother came in.

They were talking and laughing together, but their conversation was quickly stilled when Emma went to stand at the open kitchen door.

'Hello,' she said, trying not to sound as nervous as she felt. 'You're back.'

'That's my cue, surely,' remarked David shortly, levering himself back into the wheelchair. Coming up and down the steps into the house, he was forced to use his sticks, the weight of the chair with him in it being too great for a woman to cope with. He lifted his legs on to the rest one by one, and then straightened to look at her. 'What happened?'

Emma shrugged, running her palms along the sides of her arms. 'Not a lot. How—how have you been?'

Mrs Ingram had closed the door and was presently standing with one hand possessively on the back of David's chair, and it was she who answered that question with another of her own: 'Do you really care?'

'Mother!' To Emma's surprise David came to her defence. 'Leave it, will you? She's back now. We should be —grateful for small mercies.'

Mrs Ingram sniffed, brushing past him to go up the stairs. 'I'll go and pack my things, then, shall I?' she said tersely. 'You won't need me now that your *wife's* come back.'

David looked as though he might protest the truth of that, and then seemed to change his mind. Instead, he rolled his chair down the hall towards Emma, saying peevishly: 'I'm cold. Are you making tea, because I could certainly do with a cup.'

Emma hesitated only a moment, not knowing whether he expected her to kiss him or not, and then walked jerkily across to where she had left the teapot when she heard them coming in. 'I've made the tea,' she declared, taking down another cup from the rack and setting it in its saucer. 'I needed a cup, too.'

David waited while she poured the steaming liquid, then he said levelly: 'When did you get back? Mother and I have been out since this morning. We went into Stratford to do some shopping, and had lunch out.'

Emma hid her surprise. Lunches out were an infrequent luxury, and knowing the precarious state of their finances, she guessed David must have had another commission from Harry Langley. It was a relief to know that this month's bills would not be the excuse for one of those awful rows David created because of their shortage of money, and she managed to smile as she handed him his tea.

'I got back about half an hour ago,' she offered then, perching on the corner of the table. 'Has—er—has everything been all right?'

David looked down into his cup for a moment, before lifting his head and saying: 'We've managed.' Then, after a pregnant pause, he added: 'Emma, about what happened before—before you left.'

'Yes?'

Emma was wary, but David's expression was not aggressive. 'I feel I ought to—apologise,' he declared, with uncharacteristic humility. 'I—well, I guess I lost my head. I want you to know it won't happen again.'

Feeling the need to sit down, Emma dragged out a chair from under the table and sank into it weakly. 'You mean that?'

A trace of irritation crossed his face at her words, but he nodded, continuing gruffly: 'I've said so, haven't I? If you can forget it, then so will I.'

'Forget what, David?' Emma smoothed the pad of her index finger along the table. 'I'm sorry, but I don't know what you mean.'

He glanced behind him irritably, obviously concerned that his mother might reappear at any moment. 'You know,' he insisted. 'I've disposed of—of the evidence, and so far as I'm concerned, it never happened.'

Emma expelled her breath on a faint sigh. 'And the other?'

'I've said I'm sorry,' he muttered. 'Can't we—make a fresh start? Begin again? We were happy once.'

Were they? Emma doubted they had ever known that enviable state. Reasonably content, perhaps. Resigned, certainly. But happy? Happiness was something she never considered her right and privilege. And until she had discovered David's secret, she had not questioned the loyalty she had always given him.

'I—I've been thinking things over, too,' she said carefully, and saw the way his hands tightened on the arm of his chair. 'I—I'm prepared to overlook your—your relationship with—with that girl, providing you're prepared to make an effort to—to stop feeling sorry for yourself.'

'To stop feeling sorry for myself!' His echo of her words was harsh, but as if he was making a concerted effort to placate her, he eventually schooled his features and nodded his head. 'I admit I have sometimes been a little—impatient in the past,' he agreed. 'But life isn't easy in a wheelchair, Emma.'

'Life isn't easy for anyone,' she replied quietly. Then she made an offhand gesture. 'What have you been doing while I've been away? Have you finished the drawings you were working on?'

'No.' David faced her defiantly, as she bent her head in exasperation, and she said flatly:

'Then how could you and your mother afford to have lunch in Stratford? We live on a pretty tight budget, David.'

He snorted then, his earlier promise quickly forgotten. 'You're a fine one to talk, aren't you?' he snapped. 'Flying off to the West Indies at a word from the Kyles! Living it up, while I have to scrape and save here!'

'We don't have to scrape and save, David. Just watch our spending, that's all. And perhaps there's some justification in what you say. But I didn't pay for the trip to Valentia, and you know it.'

The sound of Mrs Ingram coming down the stairs again silenced any reply David might have intended to make, and instead they both looked expectantly towards the door as the older woman came to make her farewells.

'I'm leaving now,' she announced peevishly, pulling on her gloves over her plump fingers. 'I'll have to call at the shops on my way home and get something to take in with me. Living here, I haven't had time to look after my own flat.'

Emma could have said she hadn't made much of an effort to look after the house either, but she didn't. Instead, she offered her thanks for what she had done, and David joined in to suggest that his mother should take a taxi home and they'd pay the fare. As it was only about a quarter of a mile to Mrs Ingram's flat, Emma thought that was unnecessary extravagance, but she kept her mouth shut, and saw the older woman's features relax somewhat.

'That would be nice,' she agreed, smiling smugly at her daughter-in-law. 'Would you call one for me, Emma. I'll have a cup of tea while I'm waiting.'

It was as if she had never been away, Emma thought wearily, as she went to make the call, but to regain David's good humour she would have done a lot more than that.

Within three days she had restored the house to its former cleanliness, and outwardly at least she had put the past behind her. David showed unexpected interest in everything she had done while she was away, and although talking about the Kyles was painful to her, she endeavoured to satisfy his curiosity. She supposed she ought to be grateful he was treating the affair as casually, but it was so unlike him that she couldn't help a few twinges of suspicion when he showed sympathy for Jordan's father.

'You have to admit,' he said one evening, after he had drunk the better part of a bottle of claret, 'credit where it's due. Without Andrew Kyle, the Traces would have come down in the world a damn sight quicker than they did, don't you agree?'

'I didn't know you were an admirer of the Kyles,' Emma retorted tightly, covering her glass with her palm when he would have refilled it. 'You've never shown any interest in their affairs before.'

'Ah ...' David tapped his nose significantly with one finger. 'That was before I knew how—how—highly they esteemed my wife.'

'David! Honestly!' Emma rose abruptly to her feet. 'Just because Andrew Kyle wanted to make his peace with me before he died it doesn't mean they hold me in any high esteem.' She pursed her lips. 'As—as a matter of fact, I doubt if I'll ever see any of them ever again.'

David lay back in his chair and regarded her through half-closed lids. 'I wouldn't be too sure of that, if I were you,' he essayed annoyingly. 'I mean, you haven't said in so many words, but it's obvious, isn't it? The old man's dying. There might be a—a little nest-egg for you in his will——'

'*David!*' Emma was disgusted by the mercenary streak in him, and just for a moment she wondered whether he seriously believed what he was saying. Was it possible his new-found tolerance stemmed from a totally unfounded idea that Andrew's summons had had some material benefit attached? That it had, and that she had turned it down, was not relevant. She wanted no part of Tryle Transmissions, now or in the future. Her father had died owing more money than she could earn in a lifetime, and there was no way she could ever repay that debt. To contemplate taking a share of the company, that since her father's death had expanded enormously, was too much like feeding from the bones of dead men.

Gilda rang her a few days after her return and suggested she wait the week before coming in to the shop. 'Mr Peabody told me you were back,' she explained. 'He said you looked pale and tired, so if you feel you need more than the week . . .'

'Oh, no. No.' Emma's tone was urgent. 'I—I'm looking forward to coming back. I'll see you Monday as usual.'

Gilda was only too willing to agree, and with her usual tact maintained a tacit silence about Emma's trip during the first couple of days she came in to work. But inevitably Emma wanted to talk about it, and over a cup of coffee one morning she narrated the events as they happened, omitting only the details of Andrew's last encounter with her father as he had told them to her.

Gilda listened to what she had to say, and then tipped her head against the ladder back of her chair. 'You're a fool, do you know that?' she demanded impatiently. 'If Andrew Kyle wants to make you half owner of the company, you should let him. You and David are not so well off that you can afford to turn down a chance like this. And besides, it could be that Jordan's father feels he owes it to you.'

'Owes it to me?' Emma's head jerked round. 'What do you mean?'

Gilda sighed. 'Just that—well, if it hadn't been for your father, there wouldn't have been a business for old man

Kyle to put his money in, would there? And don't forget, all the connections were your father's. He had the right accent; Andrew Kyle didn't.'

Emma relaxed. For a minute she had wondered what Gilda knew, but it was no more and no less than anyone else. On the face of it, Jeremy Trace had died because he was in debt, but no one knew for how much. That was all. A common enough tragedy, in all conscience. Nothing for anyone to suspect there.

'I just don't want their money,' she insisted now, emptying her cup. 'I'm not interested in becoming an heiress, and—and working with Jordan would be—reckless, to say the least.'

Gilda shook her head. 'You say that now, because you're young—and foolish. In twenty years, you'll wonder why you ever turned it down.'

'You really believe that?'

'I do. Emotions cool. You may think you couldn't work with Jordan now, but don't you think, in the day-to-day rat-race of the boardroom, you'd stand the best chance of getting things into perspective? It's absence that makes the heart grow fonder, not familiarity.'

Emma rose to her feet. 'You may be right. But I'd rather not prove the point. Besides, if anyone should inherit half of Tryle's, it's Mummy. She suffered more than I did.'

Gilda shrugged. 'We'll agree to differ. But don't be surprised if David sees things rather differently. He's not a fool, and he must guess there was more to Andrew Kyle inviting you out there than you're telling.'

'Oh, Gilda!' Emma's eyes were wide and anxious. 'You don't think—will he be terribly disappointed when he finds out we're not getting anything?'

'Well ...' Gilda grimaced. 'Knowing your husband as I

do, I'd advise you to say as little as possible. For God's sake, don't tell him what you've turned down, or your life won't be worth living!'

It was Gilda who showed her the paragraph on the front page of the *Abingford Chronicle* a week later.

It was a bright morning, with the touch of spring in the air, and Emma, leaving the house as she usually did before David was even up, had had no time to glance at the morning paper. In consequence, Gilda's words as she removed her coat brought her head round with a snap.

'What?'

'Oh, dear, I can see you haven't read it,' remarked Gilda resignedly, folding the newspaper so that only the column she wanted Emma to read was uppermost. 'There you are.' She pointed to the item. 'I'm sorry, honey, but I did think you'd have seen it.'

Mutely, Emma took the paper from her and read the short obituary.

Andrew Kyle, retired managing director of Tryle Transmissions (Abingford) Limited, died yesterday at his home in the West Indies. Mr Kyle was a well-known figure in Abingford until he retired, an active member of the Rotary Club and town councillor for many years. His son, Mr Jordan Kyle, said his father had been suffering from cancer for some months. Mr Kyle's body is to be flown back to England for burial.

For some minutes after she had finished reading, Emma could say nothing. Then she thrust the paper aside, squared her shoulders against the ridiculous impulse to collapse in floods of tears, and faced the fact that her visit to Valentia had not happened a moment too soon.

'I'm sorry,' murmured Gilda again, her face mirroring her discomfort, and pulling out her pack of long French cigarettes, she offered it to her assistant. 'Here!' she said. 'Take one. It will help.'

Emma shook her head, but Gilda lit two and handed her one. 'Try it,' she insisted. 'At least it might put some colour in your cheeks. You look ghastly. I didn't realise he meant so much to you.'

'He—he doesn't, he didn't,' Emma exclaimed, raising the cigarette to her lips and inhaling almost automatically. Her head swam as the smoke invaded her lungs, but she managed not to choke on it, and as the fumes cleared she felt quite proud of her composure. 'He—I—it's just so sudden, that's all.'

'But you must have known how ill he was,' protested Gilda. 'I mean, Jordan told you as much.'

'I know. I know.' Emma took another pull on the cigarette, only to find her throat had not recovered from the previous onslaught and choked on a cough. 'Ugh, they're awful! How can you smoke them?' Her eyes were watering, and she was glad of the excuse to use her handkerchief. Surreptitiously, she blew her nose and dabbed away the tears that persisted in overspilling her lids, and then sniffed. 'It's just that—I never expected it to happen so quickly.'

Gilda nodded understandingly, taking the cigarette from her and pressing it out in the tray on her desk. 'Well, at least you're prepared now. Should David make a point of telling you.'

Emma felt a shiver of apprehension slide along her spine. 'They're bringing him back to England, I see. Do you think I ought to attend the funeral?'

'I should have thought it was the least you could do,'

Gilda conceded. 'After all, he never did you any harm, did he?'

Emma thought about that all through the long morning that followed. Despite her affection for Andrew, he was dead now, and she was tempted to let that be an end of it. After all, Jordan wouldn't want her there, and David was hardly likely to encourage her to get involved with the family again. Andrew had had a brother, she knew, who still lived in London, and he was bound to come for the funeral and bring his family. Then there were all the employees of Tryle Transmissions. At least a dozen of them were personal friends of the Kyles, and she could imagine how awkward they would feel, faced with Jeremy Trace's daughter. No, she decided at length, it would be easier all round if she stayed away, and made her private prayers for his soul in the anonymity of her own church.

But, to her amazement, David insisted that she must attend the funeral. He even offered to accompany her.

'He was your father's friend,' he declared, 'and he obviously cared about you. You can't stay away.'

'But David, Andrew's dead. He'll know how I feel. He'll understand. And after all, he's the only one you're concerned about.'

'I still think we should go,' insisted David firmly, and short of causing an argument, she had to give in.

But, the day before the funeral, Emma got a letter from a firm of solicitors in Stratford. She vaguely recognised their name as being the firm with which David had dealt at the time of his accident, and she couldn't imagine why they should be contacting her. She even examined the envelope again to make sure it had been addressed to her, but there was no mistake.

The letter said simply that they would like to see her, if she could call into their office as soon as possible. They gave no reason for their request, and she could hardly read the signature, but a type written definition gave the name as Horace Armitage, the senior partner in the firm.

It was one of her mornings for the shop, and David was still in bed, but instead of leaving the letter for him to read when he got up, she put it into her bag. She didn't quite know why she felt the need to hide that particular item of correspondence, but until she knew what it entailed, she decided to keep it to herself.

In fact, she was able to keep the appointment sooner than she expected. Gilda gave her the opportunity, when she suggested Emma might collect two paintings from a gallery in Evesham for her, and feeling like a conspirator, she doubled back to Stratford before returning to the shop.

Leaving Gilda's car parked near the market place, she walked the short distance to the offices of Armitage and Holland, in Chapel Street. It was a Tudor-styled building, with the jutting panes and wood facing of a bygone era, and the receptionist's office was small and unpleasantly hot from the fan heater she had at her feet. But she knew her name, and five minutes later Emma was ushered into the senior partner's office. On the first floor, this room was bigger, but redolent with the scent of old leather and characteristically dusty. The elderly man who rose to greet her matched his surroundings, she decided, but in spite of his age and wispy grey hair his smile was reassuringly warm.

'Mrs Ingram?' he said politely. 'How good of you to come so promptly. I expect you were surprised to get my letter.'

'Very surprised,' she agreed cautiously, sinking into the chair he indicated, across the cluttered desk from his own. 'Are you sure it's not my husband you want to see?'

He consulted some papers on his desk, and then looked

up at her, over the horn-rimmed spectacles which had slipped down his nose. 'Er—no, no,' he assured her. 'You're the person I wanted to see.'

'Yes?' Emma wished he would get on with it, but now that he had her here, Mr Armitage seemed in no hurry to continue.

'Yes,' he repeated slowly, shuffling through his papers again. 'Ah, here we are! Emma Jane Ingram. That is yourself, is it not?'

'Yes.' Emma's fingers tightened round her handbag. 'I—is there something wrong?'

'Wrong?' For once, the solicitor spoke without first considering his words. 'Good heavens, no! Far from it. I should say that what I have to tell you will please you immensely.'

'Really?' Emma was doubtful. What could this old man possibly have to say to her that would please her immensely? That David's insurance had been granted after all? Surely not. And besides, they would have contacted him in those circumstances, not her.

'Yes ...' Mr Armitage was marshalling his words again. 'You—er—you know a Mr Andrew Kyle of Valentia, in the West Indies, who died—let me see, four days ago?'

Emma's mouth went dry. Suddenly she could guess what he had to tell her, or rather, she thought she could, and she wanted to get up and rush out of this stuffy office before he had chance to put it into words.

But of course she couldn't do that. Rushing out of the office would achieve nothing, merely an unnecessary delay. Far better to face it now, and deal with it at once.

Mr Armitage was looking at her and realising he was waiting for her to reply, she nodded jerkily, saying: 'Yes. Yes, I knew Mr Kyle.'

'Good. Good.' The solicitor smiled. 'Well, you're a

very lucky young lady. Before his death, Mr Kyle made over half his estate to you. You would have heard of this at once, of course, but the legalities took some working out, and I myself have been liaising with Mr Kyle's solicitors in Gray's Inn. His death has precipitated matters, and I am now in a position to tell you that consequent upon the necessary forms being signed, you will be a major shareholder in Tryle Transmissions Limited, and half owner of his house in Abingford. Athelmere, I believe it's called. But I expect you know that better than I. There's a capital settlement, too, but until death duties have been paid, I can't tell you exactly how much that will be. But rest assured, it won't be less than some two hundred thousand pounds.'

Rest assured! Emma thought she would never rest assured again. This couldn't be happening, she thought wildly. Andrew could not have completed all the details before he died. Jordan had said he had been drawing up the papers. There had to be some loophole, some way she could return the shares to Jordan. She was not entitled to anything from his estate, least of all *money*.

Realising Mr Armitage's expression was one of mild anxiety now, Emma guessed she was looking as shocked as she was feeling. But she couldn't help it. It was all too much for her. And she was very much afraid that if she didn't get some air soon, she was going to faint.

Mr Armitage reached across and pressed a button on his intercom. 'Miss Lewis?' he said. 'Would you bring us some coffee, please. For two, yes.' Then he rose to his feet and went over to the lead-paned windows, throwing one wide and saying: 'Isn't it a beautiful morning? Quite warm for March, don't you think?'

Emma said nothing, breathing deeply of the draught of air that wafted into the room. Almost immediately she began to feel better, although her physical condition troubled her less than her mental one.

'Mr Armitage,' she said, as he came back to his desk again, 'I—don't want this.'

'What?' The solicitor looked puzzled. 'You can't mean——'

'I do. I don't want to be a major shareholder in Tryle Transmissions, and I certainly don't want any capital settlement.' She sighed. 'Let me explain ...' She paused. 'Mr Kyle—Andrew Kyle, that is, felt he—owed me something, but he didn't. And—and I can't take this money. It belongs to Jord—to his son.'

Mr Armitage shook his head. 'I can assure you, Mr Kyle's son is quite in agreement with this arrangement, and indeed was party to its drawing up——'

'I know that. But it doesn't make any difference——'

'I think it does. My Kyle's estate was such that to split it into two halves is no great hardship for anyone.' He regarded her gently. 'My dear, I can understand how you feel. I'm sure you were very fond of Mr Kyle, and you never expected him to repay you in this way, but surely you can't seriously think of giving it up.'

'I can,' she insisted. 'Mr Armitage, I want you to write to Mr Kyle's solicitors and explain——'

'I can't do that, Mrs Ingram.'

'Why not?'

'Well, Mr Kyle had a clause inserted in the agreement to the effect that should you wish to rescind the settlement, you must do so independently. In other words, you can't *give* the shares back to the company. They must be sold on the open market. Mr Jordan Kyle may bid for them in the normal way, of course, but——'

'But that's monstrous!'

Mr Armitage shrugged. 'From your words, I would

ascertain that Mr Kyle knew you rather better than you think. You realise that if you do decide to sell, there's no absolute guarantee that Mr Kyle's son could afford to buy.'

'Oh, *God*!' Emma twisted her hands together in her lap. 'Is there nothing I can do?'

'Yes. Keep the shares yourself. If becoming involved in the business is your concern, you could always remain a silent participant, give Mr Kyle's son your proxy vote, and let him deal with them for you.'

Emma shook her head. She could always do that, of course, but there still remained the money, and the effect it was bound to have on their lives.

A tap on the panels of the door heralded the arrival of Mr Armitage's secretary with two cups of instant coffee. Thanking the girl, Emma helped herself to sugar, and then waited until the door had closed behind her before saying: 'I don't know what I'm going to do.'

Mr Armitage sighed. 'You need a little time, I can see that. But you mustn't forget that whatever you decide will have its effect on your family.'

'Do you think I don't know that?'

Emma's tone was ragged, and he continued: 'I mean— if you don't want it for yourself, at least think of your son.'

'*My son!*' Emma stared at him as if she couldn't believe her ears. Then she shook her head again. The solicitor was old. He was getting her confused with someone else. 'I don't have a son, Mr Armitage.'

Now it was the solicitor's turn to look blank. 'But of course you do, Mrs Ingram. I—er—his name's David. That's right, David. He must be—what?—about four years old now.'

Emma felt a sick feeling in the pit of her stomach. 'I tell you, I don't have a son, Mr Armitage. You're confusing me with somebody else.'

'Mrs Ingram, if your son's died, then I'm sorry——'

'*Died?*' Emma got tremulously to her feet. 'What are you talking about? I tell you I don't have a son. I don't have any children. My—my husband's an invalid. Surely you remember that!'

Mr Armitage levered back his chair and rose to face her. 'I remember very well, Mrs Ingram,' he declared tersely. 'But you were pregnant at the time of his accident, and Mr Ingram led me to believe that his son was born some seven months later. Indeed, I arranged the settlement myself.'

Emma's legs gave out on her and she sank down into her chair again. 'What—settlement?' she whispered faintly, and his brows drew together into a disturbed frown.

'You don't know, do you?' he exclaimed, and there was an awful grimness to his voice. 'Oh, Mrs Ingram, I don't know what to say.'

Emma looked up at him dully. 'David has a son, is that it?' she asked, and his silence answered for him. 'Just tell me—what did you mean by a settlement?'

Mr Armitage's gnarled old fingers snapped the pencil he was holding. 'I believe I've said more than enough as it is,' he decreed heavily. 'I think you must ask your husband these questions.'

Emma shivered. 'Perhaps I will.' She licked her dry lips. 'But I can guess. It was the insurance money, wasn't it? The money he said he wasn't entitled to, or something.' Her head was thumping now. 'There was a girl, you see. She was with him when—when he crashed. She must have—had his child. But I didn't know. *I didn't know.*'

'My dear Mrs Ingram.' The old solicitor leant across the desk to take her hand. 'I only wish I could say the same.' He looked at her anxiously. 'Does this—does this mean——'

'I don't know what it means—yet,' replied Emma, her voice as tremulous as her limbs.

Then she pushed back her chair again and got to her feet. 'I—I must go. My—my employer will be wondering where I am. Th-thank you for—for everything.'

Mr Armitage retained his hold on her hand as she went towards the door. 'You will get in touch with me again, won't you?' he asked urgently. 'As soon as you've decided ...'

'Yes.' She nodded, withdrawing her hand gently, but firmly. 'Good—good morning.'

CHAPTER TEN

OUTSIDE, the sun was still shining and the day had really become quite warm, but Emma felt chilled. Indeed, it was difficult for her to put one foot in front of the other, but she had to move away from the windows of the solicitor's office. She stood for several minutes on the corner of Chapel Street, shivering in the breeze that tunnelled up Sheep Street from the river, and then, pushing her hands into the pockets of her coat, she made her way back to the car park.

All these years, she was thinking numbly. All these years, David had had a son, and she had known nothing about it. The money he should have received at the time of his accident had gone to subsidise the other girl's pregnancy, and while she was struggling to make ends meet, Sandra Hopkins was calling herself *Mrs* Ingram, and having his child!

There was something so cold-blooded about it somehow. To her knowledge, David had never even seen his son, although she could be wrong about that as she had been about so many things. No wonder he had been so alarmed when she discovered the handbag in the attic, and she was beginning to understand why talking of the accident had aroused such strong emotions.

Unlocking Gilda's car, she got behind the wheel, but she didn't start the motor. In the sun-warmed cocoon of the small saloon, she reviewed the events of the past few weeks, reflecting wearily that Jordan's call had been the reactor

164

that set the chain in motion, each successive link exploding the myths she had lived by. Nothing was the same any more. Even the ground at her feet seemed to have been torn out from under her, and there was no one to whom she could turn, with whom she could share her pain and bewilderment, from whom she could gain the strength to go on.

She rested her hot forehead against the smooth plastic of the steering wheel and tried to look positively into the future. But all she could hear was Mr Armitage's voice telling her that David was the father of another woman's child ...

Taking a deep breath, she reached for the ignition, but as she did so, she remembered Jordan's words in the library of his home, his reluctance to discuss the crash with her. He had implied there was more that she should know about it, and she wondered now if he had known about the child all along. It was humiliating to realise that a great number of people must know about it, not least the girl herself and her relatives.

Shaking her head, she started the engine and reversed out of the parking space. How right she had been to give in to her instincts to keep the letter from the solicitors with her that morning. If she had left it at home, she might never have discovered the truth. If Gilda had not asked her to go to Evesham ... if David had assured her the letter was really addressed to him ... if he had dealt with the affair himself ...

So many 'ifs'. Emma's fingers curled tightly over the wheel. Her life was full of them. If her mother had not had that affair with Jordan's father ... if her father had not been so willing to believe he was a loser ... if someone had not taken it into their heads to tell Jordan those lies ...

The burgeoning countryside meant little to her as she

covered the few miles to Abingford. The budding beauty of the almond blossom, the fresh young greenness of the hedgerows, made no inroads into her deadened senses, but after negotiating the traffic lights at the end of the High Street, she turned into Hunter's Mews and drove to the house in Mellor Terrace, not back to the shop.

Locking the car, she ran up the steps to the door, and inserting her key, opened the door into the hall. Cold resolution was driving her on, and she strode down the hall towards David's study, determined to tell him what she had learned. But as she reached the end of the hall, the drawing room door opened behind her, and a woman's voice said:

'Emma! Hello, darling. Did Gilda give you the message?'

Emma swung round disbelievingly to gaze at her mother standing in the open doorway. She was the last person she expected to see, and for a moment she could only stare at her, lips parted.

'M-message——' she managed to say at last, breaking off as David's chair whispered to a halt just behind her mother, and he took up the explanation:

'We rang the shop,' he said, unaware of his wife's instinctive withdrawal. 'Gilda said you were out, but that she'd let you know as soon as you got back.'

Gilda was talking on the telephone when Jordan entered the antique shop, but she recognised him at once, her eyes registering her surprise at seeing him there. She quickly finished the call and replaced the receiver, sliding off the desk to straighten her skirt. In black suede pants and a black leather jerkin, he was a disruptively masculine presence in the somewhat feminine surroundings of fragile glass and delicate works of art, and just for a moment she allowed herself the luxury of imagining he had come to see her. In spite of all her vows of self-sufficiency and independence, she knew that if a man like Jordan Kyle had come into her life, she would not have let him go so easily, but his current interest in her young assistant could only bring her more unhappiness. He was not dependable, he had proved that, and for all his faults, David had married her.

'If you're looking for Emma, she's not here,' Gilda said now, putting her hands on her hips in an unconsciously aggressive gesture, and Jordan's lips twisted.

'No?'

'No.'

'This isn't one of her days for working?'

'Well, it is. But she's not here. She's gone to Evesham to collect some paintings.'

'I see,' Jordan nodded. 'When will she be back?'

Gilda shrugged. 'I don't know.' She omitted to add that she had expected Emma back by now, or that David had already been on the phone asking for her. Her mother had apparently arrived ... unexpectedly. Although looking at Jordan now, Gilda guessed his father's funeral was the factor that bound them all together.

'You don't like me, do you, Gilda?' Jordan said now, and she marshalled all her defences against his uninvited attack.

'I—wouldn't say that,' she denied carefully. 'I don't know you well enough to like or dislike you.'

'I find that hard to believe,' he remarked dryly, making no move to go. 'In fact, I would say we knew one another reasonably well. After all, we were at school together.'

'I was older than you were,' retorted Gilda. 'We hardly saw one another.'

'Nevertheless, you've known me a great number of years.'

'If you say so.'

Jordan bent his head. 'Don't make it so hard for me, Gilda. I need your help, not your hostility.'

'My help?' Gilda was startled. Then her lips tightened. 'If you think I'm going to plead your case with Emma after what you did to her——'

'What did I do to her?' he demanded, overriding her resentment. 'What do you know about it? How can you possibly judge, when you don't know the facts?'

'I know that for Emma everything collapsed on the night her father committed suicide!'

'Her father! Yes, her father.' Jordan's mouth was grim. 'What would you say if I told you that I believed that Jeremy Trace was not her father? That *my* father was!'

Gilda gulped. 'You're crazy!'

'Am I? Am I?' He controlled himself with an effort. 'But suppose I'm not? Suppose what I said was true. Suppose the person who told me was so beyond suspicion that I couldn't help but believe—that person?'

'Then—then Emma would be your—your——'

'My half-sister, right.'

'Jordan!' She stared at him aghast. 'But you couldn't—no one would——'

'Someone did. Someone who hated my father, and used me as a tool to get back at him.'

Gilda's hands curled and uncurled against one another. 'Wh-who?' she ventured. 'Your mother? Jeremy Trace? Not—*Emma*?'

'No, not Emma. Not any of those people. Someone else. Someone who needed to hurt me, as my father had hurt them.'

'Not—not *Mrs* Trace?'

'You've got it.'

'Oh, God!' Gilda sought her desk and leant her weight

against the side of it. 'I don't believe it. I just don't believe it!'

Jordan expelled his breath on a heavy sigh. 'When you're told something—something so appalling that it appears it's driven a man to suicide, you don't argue with the facts. Why should I have doubted it, particularly as I believed Emma's mother had our best interests at heart. I did try to speak to my father, but Trace's death had shattered him, too, and all my mother knew was that something my father had told him had driven the other man to take his life.'

Gilda groped for her cigarettes. 'But what about Emma? Why didn't you tell her the truth?'

'Her mother begged me not to. She said she had lost enough—that it would destroy Emma's respect for both her and her father. And I knew it would. So I—got out of the way. I guess I thought it was the least I could do.'

Gilda lit her cigarette with hands that were not quite steady. 'And—and now ...'

Jordan shifted restively. 'Sufficient to say I've learned the truth.'

'So what do you intend to do?'

'About Emma? What can I do?' His face was bitter. 'She's married, and she appears to feel some allegiance to Ingram, in spite of everything.'

'You mean—the other girl, of course.'

'You know about that?'

'Doesn't everybody?'

'Everybody but Emma, apparently,' remarked Jordan harshly.

Gilda frowned. 'Then how do you want my help?'

Jordan hesitated. 'My father's will has made Emma half-owner of the company. I want you to help persuade her to accept it.'

'I see.' Gilda bit her lip. 'As—as a matter of fact, she

told me about it. After she got back from visiting your father. She doesn't want to take it.'

'I know.' He raked a hand through his hair. 'But when I spoke to Ingram, he seemed to think he could change her mind.'

'You've spoken to David!'

Gilda was aghast, but Jordan scarcely noticed her shocked face. 'Yes, yes. I rang him after Emma left Valentia. That was before—before——'

'—before you found out the truth about her parentage?'

'Yes.' He sighed. 'I guess I wanted to reassure myself that she'd be well taken care of. I knew Ingram would have no compunction about taking the money, and maybe I thought it would make things easier for her. She means something—special to me.'

'Oh, Jordan!' Gilda made a futile gesture. 'David hasn't told Emma you rang. I'm sure of that. In fact, she told me she was hoping he wouldn't get to hear about it.'

'You're sure?' Jordan's brows descended. 'Why not?'

'Well, because she knew if David found out, he would do exactly as you say. And she really didn't want anything from—from either you or your father.'

'Oh, God!' Jordan paced restlessly about the cluttered floor. 'But surely it will make things easier all round. I mean, it can't have been easy when they got no insurance from the accident.'

'You know about that?' Gilda was surprised, but Jordan nodded impatiently.

'Of course I knew. What insurance company would pay out when Ingram wasn't even driving the car!'

'What?' Gilda was continually astounded by the things he was saying. 'What are you talking about? Are you saying David wasn't driving the car at the time of the crash?'

She stared at him incredulously. 'But I'm sure Emma doesn't know that!'

'Then why does she think they didn't get any insurance?' Jordan demanded savagely, and Gilda endeavoured to explain:

'There was some discrepancy in the premium,' she offered lamely. 'Emma said the solicitor was very sure about it.'

'Who? Old Armitage?' Jordan made a sound of disgust. 'It's possible Ingram persuaded him to say nothing. But it was commonly believed that that was why Ingram lost all his commissions. People are funny, and a place like Abingford can still be pretty insular over something like that. I know he blamed me for drumming up feeling against him, but I had nothing to do with it. He was married to Emma, and I wouldn't have presumed to make things any more difficult for her.'

Gilda stubbed out her cigarette. 'Well, I'd stake my bank balance that Emma doesn't know,' she declared flatly. 'No wonder David doesn't like being driven by a woman!'

Jordan moved his shoulders helplessly. 'I'd better go. If she comes back and finds me here, I'll be tempted to tell her the truth, and I can't do that.'

Gilda hesitated. 'Jordan, that call I was taking when you arrived . . .'

'Yes?' His eyes had narrowed.

'It was David.'

'Oh?'

'Yes . . .' She hesitated again. 'He—er—he was ringing to tell Emma that—that her mother is here. In Abingford. She must have come down for the funeral.'

'*God!*' Jordan's mouth tightened. 'How dare she? How dare she—after all this time?'

'Maybe she wants to make amends, too,' ventured Gilda lightly, but Jordan was already reaching for the handle of the door.

'Tell Emma——' he began, then broke off. 'No, don't tell her anything. Just try and persuade her that one way or another, she's got to come to terms with her shareholding.'

Half an hour later Emma phoned Gilda, After saying where she was, she explained she had called at the house on her way back from Evesham and discovered her mother's arrival for herself.

'Well, don't worry about coming back,' Gilda averred at once. 'I'll collect the paintings myself either tonight or to-morrow——'

'No! It's all right.' Emma tried not to sound as distrait as she felt. 'I—I'll deliver them.'

'There's no need——' Gilda was beginning, when Emma replaced the receiver.

'Gilda wants me to take the paintings in right away,' she said, turning to her mother who was just emerging from the kitchen after washing up the coffee cups. 'You'll be all right, won't you? Er—David will look after you until I get back.'

Mrs Trace shrugged. 'If you must, you must,' she said. 'But I've hardly had time to speak to you, Emma.'

'I shan't be long,' Emma replied tautly, pulling on her coat again, and with a brief word of farewell, she closed the outer door behind her.

The sun had disappeared now, and although it was barely twelve o'clock, clouds were drifting across the sky and darkening the streets. It was cold, now that the sun had gone, but Emma inhaled the clean air with the eagerness of a sybarite smoking opium.

She hurried down the steps and got into the car. Gilda's car, she thought regretfully, but she didn't think the older woman would object to her borrowing it. Starting the engine, she cast one last look up at the house. Its narrow windows were like blank eyes in an unforgiving face. Shivering with the aftermath of a decision taken, she drove determinedly away.

It was late afternoon when she reached London, but she knew her destination, and guessed that Tori wouldn't be home much before five. Always supposing she still lived in Normandy Square, she acknowledged anxiously, but the card Tori had sent at Christmas had not given any change of address, so all things being equal ...

Driving in London was terrible. Unused to the amount of traffic and the confusing array of one-way streets, Emma's nerves were shredded to ribbons by the time she reached the familiar environs of the square where she had lived during the two years she spent in London. It hadn't changed much. The houses were perhaps a little bit shabbier, the paint peeling a little more obviously, but their solid Victorian appearance was amazingly reassuring to someone for whom the ordinary had become the alien and unfamiliar.

The flat she had shared with Tori was on the second floor of Number 27, and after climbing the four flights of stairs, Emma found she was praying she would be at home. Ringing the doorbell, she was reminded of those awful days after the break-up of her relationship with Jordan. Then Number 27 Normandy Square had been a bolt-hole, a refuge from the raw vulnerability of her emotions, and now it seemed that way again.

The door opened at that moment, but the smile of greeting died on her lips as she looked into the face of a strange young man. He had long brown hair, overhanging thin shoulders encased in a denim shirt. Lean hips were encased in jeans, and his feet were bare.

'Oh, I'm sorry . . .' she was beginning awkwardly, when Tori's voice called: 'Who is it? Barry, who's there?'

'Me,' said Emma reluctantly, but as the young man stood aside to let her enter, she had little choice but to enter the flat. 'Tori, it's me! Emma!'

Victoria Elliot, Tori to her friends, was an attractive brunette in her middle twenties. Like Emma, she had come to London from a provincial background, and her teaching ability was put to good use at a south London comprehensive school. She was friendly and easy-going, rarely perturbed over anything, unlike the girl she had once shared with, but their differences had complemented one another, and they had become good friends.

Now she came out of the kitchen, where she had obviously been preparing some food, judging by the way she held her hands away from her, and stared in amazement at Emma.

'By all that's holy!' she declared, a half laugh breaking her features. 'Mrs Ingram, no less! What are you doing here?'

Emma felt near to tears, but she managed to maintain a calm exterior. 'I—I was hoping you might be able to put me up for the night,' she admitted, realising there was no point in pretending with Tori. 'But—if you can't, it doesn't——'

'Hey, wait a minute.' Tori looked down at her wet hands and then, with an impatient shake of her head, dried them on the seat of her pants. 'Barry,' she spoke to the young man, 'close the door, will you? This is a friend of mine from the old days. Emma—Barry!'

Emma gave an embarrassed nod to the young man, but he just shrugged good-naturedly, as if he was used to Tori's friends turning up on the spur of the moment. Then she turned to the girl.

'It's a long story,' she said, glancing significantly at Barry, 'but I just need a bed for the night, that's all. I guess I could got to an hotel, but——'

'An hotel!' Tori sounded aggrieved. 'Of course you can't go to an hotel. You know there's a bed for you here, any time.' She looked up at Barry. 'This big hulk doesn't live here. He just acts like he does sometimes. Actually, we're engaged.' She exhibited her ring. 'We're getting married in the summer, when my parents can get down from Nottingham, but until then, the flat's all mine.'

Emma sighed. 'Thank you.'

Barry looked at her, then at his fiancée, then back at Emma again. Finally he lifted the jacket that was draped over the chair by the door, and slung it about his shoulders.

'Look . . .' he said, as Emma began to feel uncomfortable, 'I guess you two have things to say to one another. I'll go and get a drink down at the pub. I'll come back for supper in a couple of hours, right?'

'Oh, please . . .' Emma began to protest, but Tori interrupted her:

'You're a doll, darling,' she assured him, pressing a warm kiss to the corner of his mouth. 'Emma and I do have some time to make up. Bring back a bottle of wine, and we'll have it with the spaghetti, mmm?'

'Fair enough.'

Barry nodded and left them, but after he had gone, Emma felt terrible. 'You shouldn't have let him do that,' she exclaimed, as Tori eased her out of her coat. 'I feel as if I've driven him away.'

'Don't give it another thought,' declared Tori lightly. 'He'll enjoy a drink, and I must admit I'm curious to know what's brought you from the wilds of the Shakespeare country to this sordid backwater.'

'Oh, Tori . . .' Emma relaxed on to the worn cushions of the couch and heaved a heavy sigh. At least this room hadn't changed, she reflected. Still as untidy as ever, with piles of exercise books waiting to be marked occupying every available space.

'Come on, then!' Tori was inquisitive. 'Have you left David?'

Emma hunched her shoulders. 'I don't know. I don't know what I'm going to do.'

'Heavens!' Clearly, Tori had not expected that answer. 'But I thought—that is, you've never mentioned anything in your letters.'

'No.' Emma half smiled, but it was a wry illumination of her features. 'Well, how have you been?'

'Me? Oh, I'm okay.' Tori sighed. 'Emma, you can't just leave it there. What's wrong? What's happened? Why are you thinking of leaving David?'

'Don't ask me,' pleaded Emma wearily. 'I—I can't tell you. Later—later perhaps, when I've worked out what I'm going to do, then I'll write to you and tell you everything, I promise.'

Tori shook her head. 'All right.' But she was disappointed. 'How long will you be staying?'

'Just tonight.' Emma looked across at her appealingly. 'I—I have to go back tomorrow. There—there's something I have to do.'

Tori was obviously bewildered. 'If you say so.' She got to her feet again. 'Come on, I'll show you where you're going to sleep. Barry's converted the box-room into a spare bedroom, and you can help me move a mattress in there.'

'Oh, but——' Emma didn't want to be a nuisance, 'I can sleep on the couch——'

'What?' Tori grinned mischievously. 'And have you

overseeing my goodnights to Barry! No fear!' She put a reassuring hand on her friend's arm to take any sting out of the words, and added: 'Poor Emma! You really do pick them, don't you? First—Jordan, wasn't it? And now David! You make me wonder whether making that kind of commitment is a good deal, after all.'

CHAPTER ELEVEN

ABINGFORD CEMETERY was a cold and grey place that wintry March afternoon. The wind that through the night had whipped the bare branches of the elms and poplars into a fury had subsided to a chill draught that whistled round the legs of the mourners as they stood at the graveside. The ground gaped before them, and Emma, hovering at the edge of that silent gathering, felt there was something obscene about putting the mortal remains of the man she had loved and hated, and finally respected, into the ground.

'Ashes to ashes, dust to dust ...'

But was that all there was to it? she wondered hopelessly. We were born, we lived, we died; and then we returned to the earth from which we came. Like the crocuses that struggled for survival at the edge of the plot, did we just enrich the soil for future generations? It was a depressingly common philosophy when someone died. A desire to feel that one was not mortal, that beyond this life there was another; but for Emma it was more than that. It was a demonstration of the futility of fighting against one's fate. An end and a beginning, but with no more certainty than the crocuses, surviving against the odds of being crushed underfoot. That was how she felt—crushed, bruised, shattered. Trampled underfoot ...

She had come to the cemetery to pay her last respects to Andrew, avoiding the church where she knew she could not come and go unobserved. Until she made up her mind what she was going to do, she didn't feel she could face David, but she had taken the trouble to ring Gilda the night before so that she could assure both her mother and her husband that she was safe and well.

Gilda's anxiety had not helped. The family were already concerned about her, she said, and Emma had sensed all the things she had left unsaid in that statement. She had also said something else, something which left Emma feeling even more depressed. David knew about the money, about her projected share in Tryle Transmissions; and like so many other things, he had not told her.

The mourners were beginning to drift away now, and because she did not want to be discovered here, she began to make her own surreptitious departure. Mingling among the onlookers, the scarf about her face successfully concealing her identity, she melted into the belt of trees that circled the graveyard. When a hand fell on her shoulder, she almost let out a startled cry, and swinging round she stared despairingly into Jordan's face.

'Hello, Emma,' he said quietly. 'I knew you'd come. Your mother was sure you wouldn't, but I knew you would.'

'Mother? I——' Emma glanced about her desperately. 'Is she here? Of course, she must be. And David? Oh, please, Jordan, I don't want to see anyone——'

'Calm down, calm down, calm down,' he decreed, a trifle roughly. 'No one's going to make you do anything you don't want to do. Yes, your mother's here, but she's with my Aunt Agnes, and—and Ingram didn't show his face.'

'He—he didn't?'

'No. Why should he? He never had any love for my father—only for his money!'

Emma licked her dry lips, looking round apprehensively to see the groups of mourners moving towards the procession of cars that waited to take them back to the reception.

No one was paying any particular attention to them, but sooner or later Jordan was bound to be missed.

'I'm—I'm sorry, Jordan,' she said now, remembering her reason for being there. 'About your father, I mean. It was quite a shock when I read—when I read it in the paper.'

Jordan nodded half impatiently, taking her arm, and she looked up at him in blank disbelief. 'Come on,' he said. 'We have to talk.'

'No.' Emma shook her head, drawing away from him. 'No, Jordan, I can't——'

'Why can't you?'

'I just came back to pay my respects to your father, not to—not to——'

'—see me?' he asked bitterly.

'No. That is—well, yes. That was part of it.'

'Why? Because of what I said to you? Because you know I thought we were—related?'

Her eyes were wide. 'How do you—what do you mean?'

'I know,' he said softly. 'My father and I—we had quite a talk about you before he died.' He made a rueful gesture. 'Even then, I was prepared to disbelieve him, but there was one way of proving it—to myself, at least.'

'What——'

Jordan looked down at her, his dark eyes brilliant in his tanned face. 'While it's not possible to prove conclusively that one is the father of a child, it is possible to prove that one is not.' He shook his head. 'Blood groups, Emma. If only I'd checked years ago! But I had no doubts then . . .'

'But how did you——'

'I went and saw old Doctor Forrester. With a little persuasion he was prepared to tell me your blood group and that of your mother. I knew my father's already. That was enough.'

She trembled. 'So that was why ...'

'Why I walked out on you? Of course.' His voice thickened. 'How can you doubt it? We were in love. I love you still. And I think you love me.'

Emma shook her head. 'But who told you? Who lied to you? Tell me that. It—it can't have been—your father——'

'No.'

'Mine?'

'No.' Jordan raised his shoulders sadly. 'Emma, it was your mother. I'm sorry, but you deserve to know the truth.'

Emma stared back at him through a glaze of tears. 'No ...'

'Yes.' He sighed. 'I'm sorry, Emma, but it's time you knew the truth. Your mother never wanted us to marry. She never thought I was good enough for you. And—and when my father—I know you know what he said, he told me. Well, when he denounced her like that, she never forgave him. And by lying to me, she could hurt him in the most subtle way of all. She knew he expected us to marry and have children—*his* grandchildren! And indisputably hers as well.'

'But—but why——'

'You know the history,' Jordan shrugged. 'Maybe she should have married my father. Certainly she was attracted to him, and that was something she could never live with.' He shook his head. 'My father was so—uncultivated. So crude, in her eyes. It went against the grain that he should have this fatal fascination for her.'

'Fatal indeed!' whispered Emma faintly.

'Yes.' Jordan's hands descended on her shoulders. 'Now, what are you going to do?'

Emma moved restlessly. 'I suppose—I suppose I must

see David,' she admitted at last. 'I didn't want to, but I see now that I must.'

Jordan nodded. 'I won't stop you.'

Emma looked up at him. 'But what else can I do? He's still my husband. He'll never let me go, not now.'

'Do you want him to let you go?' asked Jordan quietly, and she gazed at him with her heart in her eyes.

'I never stopped loving you, Jordan,' she admitted honestly, but she evaded him when he would have pulled her into his arms. 'I tried to pretend I had. I suppose I was guilty of encouraging David in an attempt to make you jealous. But the week—the week before the wedding, I'd decided I should call it off. Then—then David had the accident, and the rest you know.'

'That's all I wanted to know,' he said softly. 'Come on. Uncle Daniel can handle the reception at the Stag. You and I will go and see Ingram.'

But at the house in Mellor Terrace, Emma faltered.

'I think I ought to see David alone,' she murmured, as Jordan would have got out of the car with her. 'Give me some time. I have to do this by myself.'

'Emma——'

'Please. I know what I'm doing.'

The door opened before she could find her key and use it, however, and Mrs Ingram stood there. She looked flushed and discomfited, as if unprepared for Emma's arrival, and Emma had the feeling that if she could she would have forbidden her the house.

'David's resting,' she said instead, but Emma only raised her eyebrows before pushing past the woman into the hall.

The hall was unnaturally hushed, as if a conversation which had been going on had been suddenly stilled. Emma sensed the presence of someone else, and instead of approaching David's bedroom, she thrust open the drawing room door. A girl of about her own age was seated on the edge of the sofa. She was small and blonde, and her clothes were smart, if a little cheap. David himself was seated close by, his face a mask of anger at this sudden intrusion, and Emma didn't need to ask the girl's name to know exactly who this was.

'Hello, David,' she said, marshalling her defences. 'I didn't know you had company. Your mother——' she glanced round at Mrs Ingram hovering anxiously behind her, 'your mother thought you were resting.'

'There's no need to be clever, Emma,' said David harshly, his knuckles white where they were gripping the arms of his chair. 'I know what's happened. Sandra's told me. I suppose you think you've been remarkably shrewd.'

Emma shook her head. 'I don't think that at all,' she denied. 'On the contrary, I've been remarkably stupid. Living with you for four years, and never suspecting——' She broke off and turned to his mother. 'Did you know? Satisfy my curiosity. Did you honestly know what had happened?'

Mrs Ingram's shoulders were heavy. 'No. No, of course not,' she replied dully. 'Do you think I would have let you marry him if I'd suspected?'

'You couldn't have stopped us,' retorted David coldly. 'Just because you've had your eyes opened now, don't think you could have altered the way things happened.'

'David!' Mrs Ingram was shocked. 'How can you speak to me like that? After all I've done for you . . .'

'What have you ever done for me?' he snapped. 'Except what suited you? Don't pretend it didn't suit you to have a tenant for this old ruin! It was far too big for you to handle alone, and Emma was always a far better housekeeper than you!'

'David!'

It was the girl, Sandra, who spoke, and he rounded on her, too. 'As for you,' he declared, 'you can get out of here as soon as you like. Don't imagine that if I hadn't married Emma I would have married you, because nothing would have persuaded me. You were an—amusement, a diversion. But that's all.'

Sandra rose to her feet then, and looked squarely at Emma. 'You have my sympathy,' she stated steadily, and without waiting for David to say anything more, she left them.

Alone with the Ingrams, Emma found she was trembling, but Mrs Ingram was staring at her son as if she had never seen him before.

'Don't you have anything to say to Emma?' she demanded. 'Like I'm sorry ...'

'Do you think she'd believe me?' David uttered a harsh laugh. 'You're a romantic, Mother. I'm a realist. I know what I'm fighting for, and it's not the same as you.'

Emma turned to Mrs Ingram. 'I can't stay here. You do understand that, don't you?'

Mrs Ingram nodded. 'What will you do?'

'Who brought you here?' demanded David, ignoring his mother. 'Did that devil Kyle have a hand in this?'

'David!' Now his mother uttered a painful cry. 'Don't go on with this. Let the girl have her freedom. It's the least you can do.'

Emma shivered. 'I don't—think he will. At least, not voluntarily.'

'The marriage has never been consummated,' said Mrs Ingram tersely, who knew her son's condition as well as anyone. 'There's always an annulment.'

'An annulment?' The idea had never occurred to Emma.

'An annulment!' echoed David mockingly. 'Now what would an annulment be worth to that rich benefactor of yours, I wonder? Ten thousand? Twenty thousand? Fifty?'

'One hundred,' said a quiet voice behind them, and Emma swung round to find Jordan right behind her.

'No——' she began, but the two men weren't listening to her.

'Are you serious?' David's lips twisted. 'Would you really *buy* a bride?'

'Jordan——'

'I'd do anything, if it meant happiness for Emma,' Jordan replied evenly. 'Were you serious? Or would you rather we waited the two years and obtained a divorce with or without your permission?'

The flames of the fire that burned in the grate cast mellow shadows over the rest of the room. After assuring herself that they had everything they needed, Mrs Govan had left them, and now Jordan pressed Emma down into the depths of one of the worn velvet armchairs in the library at Athelmere.

Then he squatted down before her and said: 'Can you relax now?'

'Will I ever?' Emma trembled. 'I—I can hardly believe it.'

'What? That you're free? Or that Ingram would take the money?'

'A little of both, I suppose. Oh, Jordan, what will he do? Even his mother has turned against him.'

'Not for long, I'm sure. She's still his mother. Once she gets over the shock ...' He shrugged. 'At least they won't starve.'

'If you hadn't come in ...'

'But I did. As soon as I saw Sandra come out, I guessed it wasn't going to be easy for you.'

Emma allowed him to take her hand then and press it against his lips. When she could speak again, she whispered:

'Poor Sandra! She's had quite a raw deal.'

'Do you think so? Even if I tell you it was she who was driving at the time of the accident?'

'Oh, no!'

'Oh, yes. Maybe Ingram had been drinking. Maybe she just wanted the chance to drive his car. Whatever, it was she who drove the car into the tree that crippled him for life.'

'Oh, how awful!'

'Yes, it must have been.' Jordan was silent for a moment. 'But even then Ingram's devious brain didn't let him down. He knew two things: first, if Sandra was discovered with him, he would lose you, and secondly, if the police discovered how the accident happened, he would lose the insurance. Somehow, after persuading Sandra to leave him, he managed to get into the driving seat, and when the police came, it looked a straightforward act of mistaken judgment.'

'Oh, God!'

'That was the end, so far as Sandra was concerned. She knew he was no further use to her, and she didn't need a lot of persuading to keep quiet about the whole affair. Particularly as soon afterwards she discovered she was pregnant, and Ingram bought her off with the insurance money. You found that out yesterday, too, didn't you?'

'But—but how did you learn all this?'

'Quite simple. I went looking for the girl.' Jordan grimaced. 'I'm not proud of what I did, but something Gilda said alerted me.'

'You've spoken to Gilda? About me?'

'Yes. Yesterday. I wanted to see you—to tell you why—I didn't know you already knew about—about what my father had said.'

'Oh, Jordan!'

'Well, as it happened, it was the best thing I could have done. You see, she told me the reason you believed you hadn't got the insurance money was because of some—technicality. That aroused my suspicions. When Gilda said that, I had to find out.'

'And you saw—the girl?'

'Eventually, yes. The boy too. He's a mischievous little devil.' He paused. 'He is Ingram's son. There's no possibility of an error.'

Emma pressed her lips together. 'What—what did she say?'

'Not a lot, to begin with. But when I explained that unless she told the truth, I was going to take all my suspicions to the proper authorities, she soon came round. Apparently Ingram threatened her with prosecution if she dared to tell the truth, and she knew she'd been committing an offence, driving the car without insurance or licence.'

'But she was pregnant . . .'

'Yes. Well, apparently she suspected it at the time of the crash. Maybe that caused Ingram to drink. He knew the risks he was running, and time seemed to be running out. She got the insurance money anyway, and that was the last she heard of him.'

'But the child . . .'

'He said he never wanted to see it. He told her never to contact him again.'

'Oh, Jordan!'

For a moment there was silence as his mouth explored the parted contours of hers, then Emma drew back to whisper:

'If your father—if your father hadn't felt the need to confess—hadn't insisted on making over half his estate to me ...'

'Ingram might have got away with it,' Jordan nodded. 'Do you think my father's earned forgiveness? For what he did to you and your mother?'

'If only you'd questioned what my mother said. If only you'd told me ...' Emma whispered tremulously. 'But if you can forgive my mother, I can forgive your father.'

'Your mother and I had quite a talk this morning,' confessed Jordan softly. 'She's quite reconciled to the fact that her strategy has failed. And perhaps, when she has grandchildren ...' He frowned. 'It's you she's concerned about. She needs your forgiveness, too.'

Emma made a helpless gesture. 'It's too late now for bitterness.'

'That's what I told her.'

'We've wasted so much time ...'

'Well, you believed what Stacey said, remember?' he reminded her gently, and she leaned forward to press her face into the hollow of his neck.

'Hmm, Stacey,' she murmured. 'What about her? What will she say when you tell her you're going to marry someone else?'

His laugh was soft. 'I'm sure it will come as no surprise to her. Besides, there's always Clive.'

'You—know about him?' Emma lifted her head, but he pulled her to him again.

'As he's one of our foremost composers, I suppose most people know him,' he said, and she realised why she had recognised the name. 'But as far as knowing about him and

Stacey is concerned, they knew one another long before I came on the scene. In fact, it was through Clive that I got to know her.' He grinned. 'I guess you saw more than you bargained for from the yacht that day. I had time to think about that, and I guessed why you kept silent. There was no need. Stacey knew that our association was a fleeting thing at best.'

Emma pulled a face. 'She didn't act that way.'

'No, well—like everyone else, Stacey likes to think she makes the running.'

Emma slid her fingers into the neckline of his shirt. 'Have there—have there been a lot of women?' she questioned tentatively, and felt the vibration of his suppressed laughter.

'Some,' he agreed, turning his lips against her forehead. 'I'm only human, and you did marry Ingram. I could have killed you for that.'

'There was never——'

'I know.' His mouth traced the curve of her cheek. 'I have had some little experience, and I'd say you were—untouched.'

'Oh, Jordan ...' His hard kiss was wholly satisfying, and as he pulled her down on to the rug beside him her whisper of contentment was the only sound in the firelit room ...

Forthcoming Mills & Boon Romances

THE RIVER ROOM *by Anne Weale*
How was Marina to cope when her wildly attractive boss made it clear that he had no objection to combining business with pleasure?

THE CRUEL FLAME *by Charlotte Lamb*
Lisa sensed there would be trouble when TV star Matt Wolfe came to live in her quiet Cornish seaside home — and she was right!

SON OF ADAM *by Margaret Rome*
It was to help her parents that Dove had taken a job in one of the Arab oil states — but Marc Blais didn't know that, and he didn't trust her an inch!

TO TAME A VIXEN *by Anne Hampson*
Beth had never forgiven Chad Barret for humiliating her — and now he was to be her next-door neighbour. How was she going to survive the experience?

TIDEWATER LOVER *by Janet Dailey*
Cole Whitfield had been nothing but an unpleasant voice over the office phone to Lacey. But then she met him, and liked the reality rather better than the voice!

SAVAGE LOVE *by Mary Wibberley*
Kim hadn't expected to meet her ex-husband Luke when she went to the Lake District. And still less had she foreseen what would happen as a result . . . .

THE LAKE OF THE KINGFISHER *by Essie Summers*
Elissa was happy to be returning to New Zealand — but the picture changed when she realised that farm manager, Logan MacCorquodale, hadn't even been expecting her!

LATE RAPTURE *by Jane Arbor*
Five years apart had not killed Cleo's love for her former husband Luc — but as he obviously didn't love *her*, what was the use of that?'

RETURN TO SILVERCREEK *by Elizabeth Graham*
Jan had parted from her husband Kyle three years ago, and she was determined to prevent him from ever learning that she had had his son.

RIGHTFUL POSSESSION *by Sally Wentworth*
Genista had taken it for granted that her marriage to Marc Kiriakos was to be in name only, but it seemed she had been over-optimistic . . . . .

Mills & Boon Romances
— all that's pleasurable in Romantic Reading!

Available December 1978 — Only 50p each

192